Mother Daughter

MOTHER
DAUGHTER

ANYA MORA

JOFFE
BOOKS

Joffe Books, London
www.joffebooks.com

First published in Great Britain in 2024

Cover art by Imogen Buchanan

ISBN: 978-1-83526-792-9

"Asking for a sign is a sign."
—Unknown

AFTER

Maple

I thought I loved him. That first time we met up, him and I, I really thought it would end in some sort of happily ever after. I thought it was all meant to be. That the conversations that brought us together were signs. Like this was one of the miracles Mom always talked about.

But they weren't signs at all.

They were warnings.

"I don't want to die," I plead, his hands wrapped around my neck. Squeezing tight. His eyes are like the ocean, dark and deep but I don't want to drown.

I want to breathe. This can't be how my life ends; before it ever really began.

"I know you want this." He smirks. Torturing me is a game he has quickly gotten very good at playing. Like he has had lots of practice with other people.

My pain runs down my cheeks, past my chin, and I know my saltwater tears are falling on his hands, the ones tight around my neck, and I hate that. It feels too intimate, too tender.

1

And to think that for a moment in time, I thought he might be the one to wipe my tears away.

"Let me go," I gasp.

He laughs. Releasing me. I collapse to the floor, my knees have gone out. I heave, panting and desperate for air. And tired. So, so tired.

"Get ready," he says. "You have work to do."

On my hands and knees, I try to stand. I see myself in the full-length mirror secured to the back of the bedroom door.

I look like a ghost. Like a memory.

How can one girl disappear so fast?

It's only been two days since I walked into this apartment, and yet my entire life has faded away.

Two days since I left the house for the last day of school. It feels like an eternity ago.

I want to go back to the last morning I was in our kitchen, when Mom asked if I wanted a piece of toast for breakfast. If I could do it all over again, I would tell her yes please. While she spread butter across the bread, I would tell her about Piper and how she also got a job working the coffee cart at the club this summer and how Jude is working at the golf course. Then, when she inevitably asked who Jude was, I would tell her he just asked me to be his girlfriend and I wouldn't get annoyed when she asked for details. I would tell her everything I knew about him, and everything else, too. Even all these messy parts that landed me here.

The man I am here with is not who I thought. He is a monster.

If Mom knew everything, then maybe she would have a clue, some way of finding me.

I would go back in time and give her all the signs I could think of.

Then maybe we would both get a miracle.

Maybe then, I would be free.

CHAPTER 1

Ruby

The words are impossible to find. Again.

Writer's block has never happened before, but this is only the second book I have ever written. The first book was the story that changed my life. I got a big advance, was able to buy a home, quit my job at *Aw, Shucks* —the oyster bar in town — and became the mom I always wanted the time to be. Cue the teenage years when my kids no longer need me to tie shoelaces or pack lunches for school.

I got that all for the low price of telling my life story. Or at least a chunk of it.

Of course, my agent sold the story as fiction because that is what I told her it was. No one would imagine the hell I went through as true. And I have never told anyone that the pages in that book reflect the hell I lived before Maple was born.

I changed my name years earlier, when I ran away, and never looked back. No one imagined Ruby Clarke was the alias of Tilly Train, and it's not like any one from my past had any interest in tracking me down.

After knocking on Maple's bedroom door, I open it and call to her to wake up, "Morning, syrup."

But she isn't there.

"Maple?" I repeat, confused. I walk to her bed and find it empty.

Normally, she would groan, burying herself deeper under the blankets, begging for five more minutes.

I flip on her overhead light before walking down the hall to see if my daughter is already in the kitchen.

I love this house. Sure, there's no air conditioning, half the windows are painted shut, and the guy who rents my basement studio apartment shouts expletives at all hours while gaming.

But I find the place charming, like a relic from my past. It reminds me of somewhere I loved. Home. Purchasing it in cash was a dream come true. The place has character.

Maple likes her best friend Piper's house more. It's new construction with sliding glass doors and a built-in microwave. And somehow, she's placed Piper's dad, Huck, in the cool category. How a local cop got that status, and I did not, is beyond frustrating.

Maybe she is with Piper. I pull my phone from my back jeans pocket and send Maple a quick text message.

Me: Morning — where are you? I know it's the last day of school but??

The text doesn't say *Delivered* which seems odd. I press call, but after several rings I give up.

Me: Please call me. ASAP.

I call Huck, Piper's dad. We don't text regularly, but I have his number saved for situations just like this.

Me: Hey, is Maple there? Or out with Piper?

A moment later, he replies.

Huck: Nope, and just asked P. She says her and Maple are supposed to meet in the parking lot in twenty minutes.

Me: Weird. She isn't here and not picking up.

Huck: I'll ask P to keep me posted. You do the same. It's the last day of school, maybe she made last-minute plans.

Me: Maybe. Thanks, Huck.

But this isn't like Maple. Piper is her only friend. I look around the kitchen, confused, remembering yesterday morning, with my daughter.

Maple held up a carton of milk. "Mom, can I still drink this?"

I took the carton from her, gave it a whiff, and told her it's fine.

"You know," I said, reaching for a loaf of bread. "Considering you point out all the reasons you find me so annoying, I appreciate you still asking for my help."

She snorted. "I was just making you do my dirty work."

"Do you want toast?"

"Nah, I'll have cereal." She grabbed a box and began to pour, then popped in an Airpod, tuning me out. Plopping in a chair at the kitchen table, she ate while scrolling on her phone. Her caramel-colored hair falls in her face, hiding her light green eyes.

I had wanted to ask who she was texting, but I held back, not wanting to become annoying and push her away. Does every mother feel like they are walking on eggshells with their teenagers, doing everything in their power to keep their perilous relationship intact?

I had asked her, "So, tomorrow is the last day of school. You ready for summer break?"

She didn't respond.

I tried again. "Did Piper get a job at the club, too?"

No answer.

I watched as she finished her cereal, stood, and put the bowl in the sink. Her black pleated skirt skimmed her butt, her purple bra straps poked out from her white cropped tank. She looked effortlessly cool in her platform sneakers and giant silver hoops.

Do mothers always have that point of realization with their daughters? That just maybe they are on the verge of becoming something otherworldly? She glowed. I looked at her yesterday and saw a walking miracle.

And now she is gone. Not answering her phone. Her best friend doesn't know where she went. The text is still undelivered.

Where is she? I scroll through my contacts, but there are no other parents to call, because Maple doesn't have friends besides Piper. Or if she does, she hasn't told me. These days I feel like I know nothing about her. And the little I do manage to get out of her, comes with commentary on how lame I am.

Dodge was never like this. But sons are not daughters.

I will never know if my own mother saw me as something holy. She died in a car accident when I was seven.

Before she left for school yesterday, she had pulled out an Airpod and told me her and Piper have orientation at their summer jobs after school. But that orientation was for today. She might skip the last day of school, but job training? She wanted this job.

Now, I look through the backdoor window, wanting a clue of where she might be. It's unsettling. I was up early this morning trying to get some writing done, I didn't hear her in the house at all . . . which means she must have left sometime in the night?

I swallow. I have kept my past a secret, but right now I wish Maple understood just how dangerous the world could be.

CHAPTER 2

Ruby

I call the attendance office at the school. "Hi, this is Ruby Clarke. Maple's mom. I was wondering if you could let me know if she made it to homeroom?"

The office attendant clears her throat. "School doesn't start for another ten minutes. And it's the last day of school, it's a little hectic around here . . ."

"Look," I say, my voice strained, needing to emphasize my point. "I don't know where my daughter is. She won't answer her phone."

The woman on the phone pauses, her tone shifting to something serious. "I will make a note to call you. But keep trying to get in touch with her. I hope it isn't like the other girls."

"Other girls?"

"Sorry, I have got to go, the last day of school is insane. But look at the paper."

"Thank you," I say as she hangs up.

It feels like a long shot, but maybe Maple has reached out to her brother. I pour another cup of coffee then give Dodge a call.

He answers his phone, which is a surprise considering he is nineteen years old. "Hey, Mom, what's up? I'm still trying to finish packing."

"Oh, I just had a quick question," I say, wishing he was already home. "I was wondering if you had heard from Maple today?"

"Uh, no, but we don't usually talk before 10 a.m."

"Right, okay, well if you do, let me know right away."

"Something wrong?"

I swallow. "She wasn't home this morning and won't answer her phone."

I hear him clear his throat. "Mom, I'm sure she's fine. It's the last day of school, right?"

I sigh, running a hand over my neck. "It's strange, she doesn't just go off the grid."

"Look, I'll be home in a few hours. I'm almost all packed up here. And I will try calling her, might have more luck as the cool older brother."

I smile. "She thinks you're cool now? That is an improvement." Last time Dodge was home Maple made a handful of teasing comments about the fact Dodge didn't have a girl-friend. Dodge took it in stride, but I remember thinking the teasing was verging on mean.

I sigh, my thoughts occupied with Maple. "I just . . . I need to find your sister. It's really worrying me."

"I'm sure you'll hear from her soon. Don't freak out, Mom. You always catastrophize."

Do I? Maybe I do . . . but I have reason to fear the worst. I have seen just how horrible the world can be, my son has been sheltered. So has my daughter.

Which is why I am so worried now.

Dodge just finished his freshman year at Pine Shore College, less than an hour away from me. It's a small private school near the state capital, tucked into a lush forest on the banks of the Puget Sound. Dodge has always loved to be in the outdoors and nature, and it felt like it fit the moment we toured campus.

I end the call with my son, then begin pacing my kitchen. I call Maple again and again. It's useless. Feeling desperate, I text her best friend Piper.

Me: Any word from Maple?
Piper: Sorry . . . nothing. Weird right?

My heart deflates. Where could she be? I decide to call Nora, my best friend. I am not one to ask for help . . . but right now I feel alone in my fear. Not knowing where Maple has gone is terrifying me.

Nora has been my best friend for over a decade. But in all that time, I could probably count on two fingers when I've actually asked for help. Once when I was having an emergency appendectomy and literally couldn't keep the kids in the hospital room with me, and the other time was when I threw out my back mid-yoga class and needed help to stand.

It's not that I don't *want* help . . . it is just a defense mechanism. Keeping people at arm's length means I can't get hurt. My trauma response is *trust no one*.

But Nora and her husband Tom have more than proved their loyalty to me over the years. Nora and I met at a book club hosted at the local library. We both loved to read, but quickly learned we loved to laugh about the eccentric members of the book group more than the books themselves. She was funny, light-hearted, and the breath of fresh air I so desperately needed. Our lives were polar opposites, she was a partner at a law office and her husband a local pediatrician, I was a single mom with two toddlers, but somehow we just clicked. She was new to the area and needed a friend as much as I did.

Early on in our friendship, long before I landed the book deal and my life changed — I was beyond broke, and doing everything I could to make ends meet for my kids. The kids and I were on food stamps and they qualified for free lunches at school. I was able to secure minimum wage jobs, but had no training in anything that would give me a leg-up. The idea of even living month-to-month seemed like a pipe dream.

But Tom and Nora were there for us then, and were willing to help financially whenever they noticed the kids needed new shoes or that I backed out of plans to meet at a restaurant because I knew I couldn't afford it. They never made it awkward or uncomfortable. They simply said it was their treat, no strings attached.

That is why when my financial situation did change, I made sure to express my gratitude.

A year ago I booked us all a trip to the Amalfi Coast. It felt like a dream come true after so much struggle. We spent a month soaking up the Mediterranean Sea and sun with Dodge and Maple, laughing and drinking Aperol and eating oysters.

But suddenly, as I realize how scared I am that something has happened to my daughter, I want my best friend at my side. I instantly regret keeping her at arm's length in so many ways, especially when time and time again she has let me in — when her and her husband Tom dealt with infertility, when she was at a cross-roads with her career, when her sister-in-law died suddenly . . . she was vulnerable with her pain and grief. I was always very aware of my inability to match her trust. Now, I need her support. A wave of fear comes over me as I stand in my empty kitchen, tears in my eyes, considering the worst.

I call my best friend as full-on panic begins to set in.

"Nora," I say the moment she answers. "Can you come over?"

"Of course, is something wrong? I'm just pulling into Hot Shots."

I imagine her in her white Land Rover, in line at the busiest coffee spot in town. I grip the counter top, needing to hold on to something as everything else seems to slip away. "Actually, yes," I say, my words shaky. "I need your help. Maple is missing."

CHAPTER 3

Ruby

I am pouring over Instagram, checking to see if Maple may have posted something in the last twenty-four hours that could give me some insight into where she may be, when there is a knock at the door.

Pulling it open, I see both Nora and Tom there, tense looks on their faces.

"Hey," I say, stepping aside and letting them in. "Thanks for coming over." Immediately I feel bad, like I am putting them out by asking for help. "Neither of you have to be at work?"

Tom gives me a quick hug. "I had the day off anyways and was over at the Juniper Lane duplex fixing a leaky faucet." He and Nora bought a duplex about ten years ago as an investment property.

Tom is an attractive man, in his early forties, with a warm smile, though a bit reserved. He is good with kids though, which is why not having any of their own was a blow for him. But his gentle nature has allowed him to be a good doctor. And though Nora says their love life has been lacking for the

12

last few years, she admits her interest has waned as much as his.

Nora gives me a big hug. "I'm so glad you called. What is going on?" She takes off her houndstooth jacket, setting it on the back of a cushioned chair in the living room and placing her purse on top of it. She is always put together, in that effortlessly cool way some people have. Her blonde highlights are always maintained, her clothing classic. All white button-downs and cropped skinny jeans with brightly colored flats or sneakers for a pop of color. This morning her canary yellow ballet flats give this dreary day a burst of sunshine.

Even with all the money I could ask for, I am still a fashion nightmare, wearing high top Vans and boyfriend-cut jeans with some hoodie or flannel shirt situation on top, a ball cap often covering my mess of hair.

I give them the run down on the morning. When I finish I ask Tom, "How was Maple after her annual checkup a few weeks ago? No problems, I assume, or I would have heard."

"She seemed fine," he assures me. "I just can't believe she's seventeen. She grew up so fast."

"Has the school called?" Nora asks.

I shake my head. "No, but I called them this morning, thinking maybe she left early this morning and was already on campus."

Tom looks at his watch. "It's only 11 a.m., Ruby."

I frown. "You think I am overreacting?"

Nora presses her lips together, the three of us sitting down on the couches in my living room. "Maybe slightly?" she says gently. "It's only been a few hours. Remember when we were outside of Rome and the kids wanted gelato and they were gone for several hours and you couldn't track their location because of spotty reception?"

I shake my head, agitated at the memory. "They took three hours to get ice cream. In a foreign country. They could have been kidnapped." They don't understand my trauma around the topic. If they did, they would be compassionate, more than that — they would see me in a new way. A way I don't want to be seen or known. Not now, maybe not ever.

"They weren't kidnapped though," Tom says calmly. "They came home laughing, had a great time. I am guessing Maple is doing the same now. It's the last day of school, she's a good kid. She is probably letting loose for the first time in her life."

It doesn't track with the Maple I know though. And even though our relationship has had its bumps the last year or so, I still know her best in the world. Don't I?

"You know, I think . . ." Nora starts but then stops, she seems to change her mind before starting again, "Have you been tracking the story of the other two girls from the high school who went missing a week ago?"

I frown, recalling the comment earlier from the office attendant. "What do you mean the girls who went missing?"

Nora pulls out her phone and begins typing. "In the last week, two girls from school have gone missing."

"What are you talking about?"

Her eyebrows lift. "You really don't read the paper?"

"You know I don't," I say. She smirks, knowing I scroll Facebook and Instagram incessantly, but those aren't exactly news sources.

"Well, two girls from the high school have gone missing," she informs me. "And I didn't know if Maple talked to you about it at all."

"No, she didn't say anything, but maybe she knows them?"

Tom pipes up. "I'm sure she does, the school isn't big." He stands. "I'm gonna go grab us some lunch. Sandwiches from the deli downtown, okay?"

I nod and Nora reaches out and squeezes her husband's hand. "Thanks, honey."

It is the sweetest interaction I have seen them exchange in months. When Tom leaves, I ask her what is up.

"What's up with what?" she asks.

My eyes widen. "With you and Tom. Since when do you *'Thanks honey'* him?"

14

She shrugs, tucking her hair behind her ear. "I am putting in more of an effort. I started going back to therapy, maybe there are things I can work on to improve my marriage. I don't want to blame our problems on him. We've been married thirteen years, maybe it's time we recommit."

I lift my eyebrows surprised. "That's noble of you. Some people might just throw in the towel."

She shakes her head slowly. "Tom is my whole family, Ruby. I don't really have a relationship with my mom, my dad died when I was young . . . we never had kids and I'm an only child. Tom has been my rock, and we've built a life together."

Now it's my turn to reach for her hand and I squeeze it. "How are you so perfect?" I tease.

She groans. "I'm hardly perfect, Ruby. Compared to you."

"Me?" I snort.

"Yes, you. You're practically a saint. A devoted mom and friend, I've never heard you raise your voice and get mean."

"What good has it done me? Maple literally cannot stand me. Which makes it all that much worse that I don't know where she is."

"I'm scared it is connected somehow to the other missing girls, Ruby. Maybe we should call the police."

"I think you're right. I can call Huck, Piper's dad."

"I forgot he's a cop."

Before I call him though, I ask, "Who are the other missing girls?"

"Lochlan and Brittany . . . but I don't remember their last names. I'm sure I can find it in the *Gazette*."

My eyes widen. "They were both cheerleaders, I remember Maple did soccer with them in middle school."

Nora twists her lips. "I heard from my coworker, Liana, that the girls have a reputation."

"Okay . . ." I say slowly. "Like a reputation for being outstanding students?"

She cringes. "More like . . . I guess they might have reputations for being promiscuous."

"Is that a word people use these days?" I ask my best friend.

"I don't know. I'm just repeating what I heard from someone at work." She sighs. "What shitty thing for adults to be discussing though, a young women's choices with her body."

"God who are these people, talking about teenage girls' alleged promiscuity?" I roll my eyes. "Look, I don't have patience for this. I am not going to get into something about these girls' reputations. It's none of our business. I just hope they were being safe and using protection. Heck, that's why I got Maple on birth control last year."

"I know," she says. "I remember that. I just hope that wherever Brittany and Lochlan are they are safe. They've been missing for a week."

I swallow, fear rising within me. "I know you and Tom think I'm overreacting, but I'm scared, Nora." Tears fill my eyes and I know this display of emotion catches Nora off guard.

"I shouldn't have said that," she amends. "They say a mother's intuition isn't to be messed with. Take it as a warning sign and call the cops."

CHAPTER 4

Ruby

I send Huck a text while we wait for Tom to return with the sandwiches.

> Me: *Hey, I can't find Maple. Getting worried.*

He immediately responds.

> Huck: *Are you home?*
> Me: *Yes. She wasn't here this morning, no word since. Not like her.*
> Huck: *I'm on my way over.*

Both men arrive at my place at the same time. Huck, the single dad of Maple's best friend Piper, is also the most handsome man I've met in years.

But right now, his looks are irrelevant. I tense, feeling too connected to criminal activity to be speaking to a local cop. "Hey," I say, "thanks for coming over. Have you met Tom or Nora?"

"I'm Huck, good to meet you both," he says, shaking Tom's hand before the four of us head into the kitchen with the to-go bags Tom has brought back. Just then I hear a car pull into the driveway. I look out the kitchen window and see Dodge's car rolling up to the house.

"Is he home for the summer?" Nora asks.

"Yeah, he got a job at the country club, same as Maple, and Piper Anne," I say.

"And Jude," Hucks adds.

"Jude?" I frown, not placing the name.

"Maple's boyfriend?" He shrugs. When my frown turns to a scowl he adds, "I could be totally wrong on that. I am just the dad of the best friend."

Nora pipes in sensing my unease, resting a hand on my arm as Tom unpacks the sandwiches and chips. The mere thought of eating makes me ill. "Ruby, it's just her age. It's not personal."

I scoff. "Except Maple is missing. If I don't know about a boyfriend, what else don't I know?"

Dodge walks in through the back door in the kitchen. "Hey, guys!" He gives the kitchen full of people a shy smile.

I give my son a hug, then stand back to take him in. His long hair is longer than it was four weeks ago when I saw him last. He's growing out some sort of goatee and mustache. There's a gold chain around his neck with a cross, it's gaudy and ridiculous, and he's wearing a pair of black silk harem pants, Teva sandals and a Carhartt T-shirt. If this is a vibe, I don't understand it. Gen Z is beyond me.

Still, my son is home. Here.

I give him another hug, before he notices the sandwiches and steps away from me to grab one.

"So what's the word with Maple? Have you heard from her?" he asks, digging into a sub.

I lean back on the counter, filling my son and Huck in on what I know. Which is basically nothing.

"The thing is," I add for Dodge's benefit, knowing Huck already knows this information, "other girls from school have gone missing too."

"Wait, what do you mean? Who?" Dodge asks.

"Lochlan Crane and Brittany Montgomery," Huck fills in.

"Wait, I know those girls from school. Jared from baseball used to go out with Brit. She was hilarious." He pauses. "Wait, so they are like missing for reals?"

Huck nods. "We've been looking for them for about a week. Considering they are the same ages as your sister, and also local, I need to go let my supervisor know that Maple's whereabouts are also unknown."

"What can we do?" Nora asks.

Huck looks at me. "If it was Piper Anne, I'd start looking. Everywhere. And talking to everyone."

"Like this guy Jude?" Tom asks.

Dodge speaks up. "Who's Jude?"

"Apparently, Maple's boyfriend," Tom says.

I look at Huck. "Call Piper Anne and ask her to come over?"

Huck nods, "Of course. School was early release today, with it being the last day of school, so they should be out of class by now. And I'll tell her to bring Jude along."

"And what will you do?" I ask.

"I'll head to the station to get everyone in the loop."

Huck leaves a minute later, and so does Tom. "I can come back any time, I just have a few things to check in on with work."

"No," I tell him. "Go."

Nora gives her husband a quick kiss. "I love you," she says.

"Love you too. Now, be a good friend and make sure Ruby eats. It could be a long day."

His words feel ominous, and I say as much after Tom leaves. Dodge shakes his head, reaching for a second sub sandwich. "I don't feel good Mom, none of this makes sense. Maple has been acting different the last few months. When would she ever leave the house without telling you . . . Or that she had a boyfriend?"

Boyfriend. "I need to talk with him."

"Sounds like Piper Anne knows him," Nora says. "Why don't you text her for his number?"

A few minutes later I get a reply from Piper Anne. I read it out loud to Dodge and Nora. "She says she's with him right now, at the job orientation at the country club. But can come over here after, in like an hour." I look at Dodge. "Should you have been at that orientation?"

He shakes his head. "No, I worked there the last two summers." He pauses. "Besides, Mom, I couldn't be there anyway. Not until we know where Maple is."

My heart tightens and tears fill my eyes as I take in Dodge's words. Where is Maple? She can't be gone. Even though she is seventeen, she is still so young.

Nora reaches for my hand, squeezes it. "We are gonna find her."

I look between my son and best friend, nauseous at the reality that my daughter has gone missing, and feeling like I just went back in time.

Only this time it isn't me who went missing. It's my little girl.

CHAPTER 5

Ruby

It's not long before there is a knock on my front door. I open it, revealing Piper Anne. There is a shaggy haired guy behind her.

Piper is beautiful with light hair and blue eyes. At heart, she's the art kid, the quirky girl with a rainbow outlook on life who wears flowers in her hair and brings sushi for lunch.

Maple's not like Piper, yet somehow those two are peas in a pod. Maple has always been less sunshine and unicorns and more black crows and full moons. They're opposites, Piper and Maple. But sometimes opposites attract.

"Hey, Ruby," Piper says, walking inside and giving me a hug. "Did you find anything out about Maple? We still haven't heard from her."

"Not really," I say. "Hi." I offer my hand to the young man I'm assuming is Jude. "I'm Ruby, Maple's mom. This is my friend Nora." Nora gives him a friendly wave.

"Good to meet you," he says, shaking it back. His handshake is firm, and he meets my eyes. The fact he doesn't look away endears him to me immediately. His hair is long around the ears and needs some sort of haircut or trim, but his eyes are clear and his soft smile appears genuine. I wonder why Maple never mentioned him to me, why she didn't want me to know about any of the things going on in her life. What was my daughter hiding?

Dodge walks into the living room. After quick hellos, he asks Piper Anne how the orientation went at the country club.

"Pretty good, just strange without Maple there . . . she was the one who insisted all of us get jobs there this summer."

I tense. It reinforces how out of the ordinary this is. It isn't like Maple to flake out, is it? "Is this your first summer working there too, Jude?"

He nods, all of us walking toward the kitchen in the back of the house. I reach into the fridge and grab sodas, setting them on the kitchen counter as he talks.

"Yeah, my first summer there. And I know getting this job is a lucky break. They don't usually hire kids like me."

"Kids like what?" I ask, trying to understand.

He shrugs, reaching for a can of Coke and popping it open. "You know, the skateboarding guy from the other side of the tracks. Not at the club, not where polo shirts and visors and Nikes are the uniform. When I wasn't working there, before I got this job, I was pretty much wearing beat up Converse with a band T-shirt. Now, I'm trying to look the part."

"Do you think you'll like it?" Dodge asks. "Being a golf caddy?"

"For sure." Jude nods. "I want to make connections, make a better life for myself."

I look at him with appreciation. He is honest, true. "Is your life now hard?"

"I'm not trying to be mean, but my dad is never happy, and always looking for a fight. I want more than that."

Piper Anne speaks up. "Maple says your dad is funny. She likes him."

Jude smirks. "He thinks Maple is cool, but he doesn't warm up to most people like that."

22

"How long have you and Maple been seeing one another?" Nora asks, piping up.

Jude and Piper Anne share a look, seeming to ask how much they should share. Jude laughs though, "Honestly, no idea. Maple gives me mixed signals all the time. One day she seems into me, the next, the cold shoulder, like she has better people to hang out with. Which is why I'm worried now . . . who are the 'better people' she wanted to be around?"

Piper Anne twists her lips, reaching for a sparkling water and opening it. "I have no idea who else she is friends with. But it's like Maple seems torn. Like sometimes she thinks Jude is awesome, and the next like she has better people to hang with."

"What people?"

"That's the thing, Ruby, I don't know. She likes secrets."

I look at Piper Anne, surprised at her transparency. "Was Maple dating other people?"

She shrugs, her voice growing quiet as she fingers the hem of her tee-shirt. "I don't know . . . like I said, she's private, keeps kinda quiet, ya know? So maybe? Just makes me wonder if we were as good friends as I always thought."

"You've always been best friends," I say, trying to soften the moment, not expecting Piper Annes reaction.

"Sure, but people change and forget to tell each other, you know?"

How many things have I forgotten to say, omitted for my own self-preservation? Too many to count. I look over at Nora who is shaking her head. "She wasn't always like that. She's always full of laughter and a little goofy. Remember in Greece how she kept making us do those relay races on the beach?"

"That was over a year ago," I say. "And Piper Anne is right, all school year she has been different. She used to tell me everything, now I can't get a word out of her."

Jude speaks up. "Even so, the girl's way out of my league. Way out, obviously. I mean, some people think she's a bit of a snob, but when you get to know her one-on-one, it's clear that it's all just a front. She's trying to keep some armor up, protect herself, you know? But I feel like when she's with me, and maybe I'm totally wrong about this, but it feels like, I don't know, she *can* be real?"

"I feel like that too," Piper Anne admits. "But then it's like days go by and she is lost in another world, totally MIA."

"Like today," Jude says. "We were supposed to be meeting up at the orientation for the summer jobs we all got. But she's nowhere."

"So when is the last time anyone saw her?" I ask.

Jude scratches his head looking around. "I haven't seen her since . . . yesterday?"

"I saw her this morning, but it was before school started," Piper says. "I've been texting her a bunch. It's so weird. She left campus before first period and I thought she was going with you."

Jude shakes his head. "It wasn't me."

"Who was it then?"

He shrugs. "I don't know, but I wish it were me."

Piper rolls her eyes. "Obviously, you wish that."

"Is it that obvious?"

"Yes, it's that obvious." Piper smiles.

Dodge cuts in. "But aren't you guys together?"

"I'm not sure."

"Why is that, you think?" Nora asks. "Do you think she might be seeing someone else? Someone she could be with right now?"

The teenagers both shrug and I wonder if they have had their fill of opening up to adults. I am surprised they said this much, but I know they both care about Maple, they must realize that this is out of the norm, especially with the other missing girls.

"It's weird though, for her not to show for orientation," Piper says, leaning into the kitchen counter. "Maple really wanted this job. We both did."

Jude shrugs. "We all did."

"Right," Piper says. "Because you're her boyfriend."

"In my dreams at least," he says with a laugh. Then he looks at me. "Sorry, I wasn't trying to be disrespectful."

"No, I appreciate you guys talking to me at all." I sigh, running a hand through my hair, wanting to keep the conversation on track. "Your dad was here, Piper Anne, and I think it is more serious than Maple skipping out on orientation. I think something might be very wrong."

Dodge clears his throat. "Look, Maple has always been her own person, she keeps her cards to herself, and likes to keep certain things private. I'm not saying we should go full on spy mode, but we need to find out if she was living some double life, you know?"

My heart pounds at my son's words. Like mother, like daughter. How much of this is my own doing? Have I been keeping as many secrets as my little girl?

"I agree," Piper Anne says. "With Maple, you think you're penetrating the hard shell she wears, but it's always just a crack. Never a big break."

Nora frowns. "I thought you guys had been best friends since middle school."

"We have been," she says. "We're always together. It's just, I don't know. She's quiet, you know?"

"She may have been quiet but there had to be a good reason, in her mind, to leave campus before school got out on the last day, without telling us where she was going, and not coming to orientation," Jude says.

Tears fill Piper Anne's eyes. "I'm worried because of the other girls."

"Lochlan and Brittany?" Dodge asks.

Piper Anne nods. "Yeah, exactly."

"I don't think Maple was friends with those girls," I say. "But maybe I don't know anything about her. Maybe I'm an idiot."

Piper looks at me pressing her lips together, squinting. "Lochlan and Brittany were partiers. I've never even seen

25

Maple drink a beer. So maybe she's just with that guy," Piper says slowly.

"What guy?" Nora asks.

"I don't know who. The guy she left school with."

Jude scoffs. "I'm the real idiot. I thought I'd been dating Maple for the last three weeks, but guess the jokes on me. You know, it kinda tracks. She's always hard to pin down. I'll say things like, 'Hey, let's meet for burgers at the Shake Stand on Friday night, six o'clock?' She'll tell me, maybe. Or when a new movie came out, I thought it could be a thing, holding hands, maybe even a kiss. She said she didn't really like romantic comedies, which honestly, neither do I, but what teenage girl says that?"

I look at Piper Anne. "Did she tell you why she would blow Jude off? Did she have other plans?"

Piper Anne shrugs. "Like I said, I don't know." She starts crying, shaking her head. "I don't know anything. She's my best friend, but honestly, it's like do I know her at all?"

I begin to cry then too, Piper Anne's tears have brought my own emotions to the surface. Nora rubs my back, comforting me as my shoulders shake.

It is Dodge who takes control. "Mom, you have to get a grip. Huck left to file a missing person report. But you can do something too."

"Like what?" I ask.

"You're a mother living in the twenty-first century. Use it to your advantage. What does her location say on her phone?"

I look up, meeting my son's eyes. I register his words. Realizing there is something to them.

"Oh, my God, you're right. Sometimes I feel so old," I say, pulling my phone from my back jeans pocket and tapping it a few times to bring up Maple's location, thankful I insisted on her sharing her location ever since she got her driver's license. "I'm so stupid for not thinking of this earlier," I say.

"You're not stupid," Dodge starts. "You're just—"

"Don't finish that sentence." I bite my bottom lip as the map reveals my daughter's location. Maybe this was all a misunderstanding. Maybe she has a good reason for leaving school today and not answering her phone. Maybe it is all going to be okay.

"So where is she?" Jude asks.

I exhale, relief flooding me. "Apparently, she's at Eagle Crest Park."

Piper Anne frowns. "That's not too far from here, right? Just a couple of miles?"

"Just over the bridge, which means she isn't missing. She's right there," I say, pointing to my phone screen. "Do you guys want to come with me? If she's there and not answering, maybe she fell or something and got hurt; sprained an ankle or has a concussion. I mean, actually, it could be pretty bad. There is a really steep trail that goes to the waterfall at Eagle Crest."

"Of course I want to come," Piper Anne says.

Jude shakes his head. "My dad is already expecting me; he gets mad when I'm late."

"Do you need a ride?" Piper Anne asks.

"It's fine, I can walk."

She frowns. "Your apartment is over five miles away," she says.

"How about I give you a ride?" Nora offers. "You two go to the park and, Dodge, you hold down home base. I will call Huck and Tom, and give them an update."

I appreciate my best friend helping make the plan. Right now I feel like I am teetering on the edge of collapse. All that matters is finding Maple. I don't want her missing like Brittany and Lochlan. I need her home.

And then I will tell her everything.

My secrets may no longer be protecting anyone. Not even myself.

A few minutes later I've said goodbye to Nora and Jude, and Piper Anne and I are in my car.

"Thanks for coming with me," I say to her as we buckle up.

"I don't really want to be by myself right now," she admits. "My dad is working, and I like being with you. It doesn't really feel safe to be alone right now. You feel safe."

"I don't think I'm doing a great job of making my house feel very safe these days, Piper Anne. Maple rarely talks to me. And I never even knew about Jude."

Piper Anne shakes her head. "I don't think that's a big deal. She wasn't sure about him. He is cool, but I'm not sure Maple really wants a boyfriend. I think he is like a comfort blanket, the kind of guy who adores you so you don't want to let go of it. Even if you don't really have romantic feelings. I think Maple wants an epic love story, the kind she reads about. I think she wants to be swept off her feet."

I look over at Piper Anne. Her sincerity moves me. That in and of itself feels like a miracle. In sharing herself, I am learning about my daughter.

And the things I learn frighten me. She may be more like me than I ever realized.

As I've been learning about miracles, I've discovered a few things. When it boils down to it, a miracle is just a synonym for love, and that's really what I'm after. Looking for glimpses of love everywhere I go. Maybe my daughter is looking from the same thing.

Trouble is, when you are young, you can look for love in all the wrong places and get yourself in trouble you aren't emotionally prepared for.

Piper Anne rolls down the window, the warm air of the start of summer sweeping into the car and bringing me back to the moment.

"Thank you for being here," I say gently.

"Of course," she says. Her words are effortless, but that is how Piper Anne has always been, sweet and optimistic, a breath of fresh air kind of girl. She has her face toward the sun, it's June sixteenth, and it should be the start of a fun few months, but suddenly it feels heavy and dark.

"You know, it's a blood moon tonight," Piper Anne tells me.

"I did not know that. Are you into planets and astrology, that sort of thing?"

She shakes her head. "No, but Maple is. She's always sending me DMs about Mercury being in retrograde."

"And what do you think about all that?"

"I think it makes my best friend really happy."

I smile. "Well, it sounds like she's lucky to have you."

Piper Anne laughs. "Yeah. Well, I really hope Maple is happy to see you in a few minutes."

I drive the car into Eagle Crest Park and find a spot to park. Together, we get out of the car and begin to follow the location on the phone. Eagle Crest Park is a nature preserve with winding trails in dense forests. There are signs identifying the local wildlife, and it is a park I have been to hundreds of times over the years. When the kids were little we would take nature walks here, collecting pine cones and leaves, pointing out mushrooms growing on mossy logs.

I wish I could turn back time to when Maple and Dodge were little. If I had the chance I would do so much differently. For starters, I would hold them closer, longer.

Now, I practically run toward the pin on my phone, both Piper Anne and I calling out for her as we walk the well-maintained trail. It's a quarter of a mile in, so it doesn't take long to get to the location. Once there, we circle it, but there is no Maple.

We look in the shrubs, around the fallen branches, the composting leaves, searching for her. Hands dirty we shake our heads, frustrated with the dead end.

"Maple would never go somewhere without her phone," I say to Piper Anne. "Maybe she just turned her phone off after coming here?"

"Yeah," Piper Anne says. "Should we keep walking the trail a little bit to see if she's here?"

We keep calling out for her, but there's no answer, my voice grows hoarse, the echo growing desperate with each attempt, both Piper Anne and me shouting into the void.

We walk toward the waterfall, and the trail ends. It's only a mile hike to the falls, a quick pay off to this natural oasis. But the rushing spring water feels too fast, like everything is about to start crashing out of control. I look over the edge of the trail, wondering if my daughter is wading in the pool below the fall.

But there is no little girl splashing about, instead the past clouds my eyes, visions of Dodge and Maple down there in the height of August, years ago, swimming in that hole, me on a picnic blanket, reading a book as the summer heat filtered through ferns, etching delicate memories on my skin.

"I don't see anything," I say. "Not even footprints. And it hasn't rained for days."

Piper Anne twists her lip. "Maybe you should call my dad."

"I will when we get back to the car. I wonder how serious anyone will take this. She hasn't even been missing for half a day," I say, not wanting my newfound hope to be dashed so quickly.

"Yeah, but think about the other girls who went missing, it's scary, Ruby."

"You really think Maple could have gotten wrapped up in whatever that is?"

Piper Anne shrugs, looking toward the dense forest surrounding us. "I don't know, Ruby, but three girls from the same town missing in a week seems pretty bad."

We get back to the car, and while Piper Anne texts Jude an update, I call Huck. "Hey," I say. "We need to talk."

"Of course," he says. "Do you want to come to me? Or I can be at your place in maybe ten minutes."

"I'm going to stop at my house, but I'll come to your house right after. I have Piper Anne and she needs to get her car."

"Are you okay to drive?"

"I think so," I say, my voice breaking. "But I'm scared, Huck. I think Maple is really gone."

30

BLAMELESS BUT BROKEN
by Ruby Clarke

CHAPTER 1

Her eyes were amber, like the stone in the pendant she wore around her neck. It was a talisman, she'd say if anyone asked. No one ever did.

She'd been on her own for too long, ever since her grandad died of a heart attack. She'd been sixteen, and he was teaching her to drive his Dodge Chevy, a car he loved more than anything, besides her. When he started clutching his chest, she knew something was wrong. She put the truck in park and jumped out of it, running down that maple tree-lined street to the first house she saw.

It was Ms. Baker's place. Ms. Baker didn't like her all that much, mostly because she was a sassy teenage girl living in a big old farmhouse with a grumpy old man who drank too much and talked too much, and didn't work hardly enough. But right now, Lucy didn't care what Ms. Baker thought of her or her grandad or anything. She needed a phone.

"Call 911." Lucy shouted from the front porch, "It's Grandad. I think he's having a heart attack."

Ms. Baker moved into action, and even though she was a busybody who always was doing 'the Lord's work' for the church, she did seem to know, deep down, right from wrong, and she was able to put aside her feelings about what she thought about Grandad.

An ambulance came a few minutes later. Ms. Baker stood there with Lucy silently. Both of them watching as Grandad was put on a stretcher, lifted into the ambulance.

"I'm going with him." Lucy turned to Ms. Baker. "They'll let me, right?"

Ms. Baker nodded, "Yes, dear. You're family, I think they'll let you."

And so Lucy got in that ambulance, and she rode to the hospital one town over, with her grandad, and while there were many things to dislike about living in rural Tennessee, one good thing about this place was people didn't ask too many questions. They just nodded at her, the paramedics, and let her get in.

She held her grandad's hand while they put an oxygen mask on top of him, pumped his heart, kept trying, kept trying. She looked into her grandad's eyes. "I love you so much," she said. He couldn't say anything back.

She knew it was just about the end of the man who was the only one left she could call family. She knew it was nearly over when he squeezed her hand, and tears filled her eyes because even if he could speak right now, he was never much of a talker. Even if he wasn't wearing that oxygen mask he wouldn't have said 'I love you to the moon and back', nothing sentimental like that.

But Lucy didn't need that. His hand in hers was more than enough. Because when you really knew someone, words didn't matter all that much. Actions did. And his actions toward her had always been pure love.

She never even knew her grandma, though the blue ribbons in the sideboard in the dining room told Lucy that she made the best bread and butter pickles in the county.

Her parents? They were gone in a car crash when she was seven, though the stories she heard made her wonder if maybe it was a good thing they were gone. She'd been staying with Grandad long before he was her official guardian. Her earliest memory was being pushed in a red wheelbarrow, bouncing through a corn maze, Grandad at the helm, steering her adventure.

It'd been nine years since she'd moved in with Grandad full-time, and it wasn't long enough. She'd want nine times as many years, nine years more times infinity, times forever, because Grandad may be a bit of an alcoholic, but he also knew how to make her laugh, knew how to make her smile.

And then, before they even made it to the hospital, he was gone.

After that day, she went back to the farmhouse that had been paid in full. And when a social worker stopped by, she said, "Don't worry about me none, I'm grown. I turned eighteen last month."

The social worker had questions, but not enough of them. Maybe there were no foster homes for a girl her age. When that social worker walked away, Lucy knew she wasn't doing her job right, but she also knew it was kind of a gift, some sort of miracle.

The hole in Lucy's heart, though, was big. Huge. And as time went on, then as years went on, it only got bigger.

The hole in her heart grew as big as that meteor she'd learned about in history class back when she was in seventh grade and was still paying attention. She stopped doing that the last few years. Mostly because she'd started talking to boys, and boys liked her. They liked everything about her. Her long brown hair, her chocolate brown eyes. One time, a boy said her eyes were like milk chocolate that they could melt right into them, and Lucy laughed at him, and kissed him and climbed on top of him. That's how it went for Lucy from then on forward until she met Knox.

Knox wasn't like the boys from school. He was older. He was dirtier, and not just the grease under his fingernails from that motorcycle he was always working on. There was a look in his eyes that said he knew danger. And Lucy wanted that.

She wanted to feel something again because she hadn't felt much ever since Grandad died, and sleeping with all those boys from high school didn't do anything. She'd gotten a job at the diner by then. She was serving plates of flapjacks, glasses of orange juice, and cups of coffee to people who came through the truck stop. Knox wasn't driving a truck. He was on a bike, and she watched him pull in. She remembered biting her lip, thinking, "Damn, that's someone who could destroy me." Which was exactly what she was after.

By then, Lucy was twenty-one years old. She felt like she was doing all right because she wasn't pregnant yet, like a lot of the girls from her high school. But when he walked in, she had this ridiculous notion that she wouldn't mind so much getting knocked up by him. Maybe it was wrong to think that way, to think that maybe she would tie that man to her by carrying his baby.

But she also didn't care because the moment he opened his mouth and asked her for a BLT, she was smitten. He knew it too. And she knew he knew, and neither of them cared.

He took her out after work for a ride on his bike. "You live around here?"

"Not too far," she said, clinging to his waist as they flew down the highway. "Three miles east."

It was a hot summer day, and her hair blew in the wind, and she held him tight, and he smelled like a man, like scotch and gasoline and leather. They pulled up to the farmhouse.

"You live here all alone?"

She nodded. "Yeah, have for a while now. It was my grandad's place."

"And where's he?"

Lucy shrugged, "Six feet under."

"You don't sound so sad."

Lucy smirked. "I figure I'm not going to show all my cards to a man I just met."

Knox chuckled, "Are you going to invite me inside?"

"Depends."

He was still sitting on his bike, and she was standing on the bottom step of the porch. Her dress was to her mid-thigh, she knew a man like him would run his fingers under it, grazing all of her. She wanted that.

"What does it depend on?" Knox asked her.

"I don't know anything about you. You could be a psychopath, a murderer, a drug dealer."

"Do I look like a drug dealer?" he asked.

She shrugged, "You don't look like a preacher."

"But I have asked forgiveness for all my sins."

Her eyes narrowed. The guys she'd been with before, they weren't real trouble. They were ridiculous. They were young and naive and thought they had all the time in the world. They hadn't experienced loss. They hadn't experienced death. They hadn't experienced that deep pain in your belly when you know there's no one in the world who's looking out for you, who even gives a damn if you live to see another day. That's a weight that was heavier than that amber necklace she still wore around her neck.

"So," he asked. "What's the verdict?"

"Where you coming here from?" she asked him, thinking maybe she ought to ask him a few questions first, before she let him inside her home.

"I come from the other side of the tracks."

She laughed, "That's pretty vague, Knox."

"You want me to be explicit?"

She licked her lips. "Yes."

"I come from a place like you've never seen. And sure, maybe you've seen some hard times in your day, Lucy, but not like me. I watched my dad kill a man when I was ten years old. I watched my brother die of an overdose."

"And your mother?" she asked him.

"She was blameless. For a while at least."

"And then what?"

"And then she broke."

Lucy knew then that there were warning signs. Everything about this man was a red flag.

She didn't know who Knox was. He came into town late at night. He wouldn't answer her questions directly. He made her feel like he was washed in trauma, bathed in it. Like everything about him was danger. But by then she was tired of trying so hard to keep it all together. Her heart had been broken by losing everyone who was a part of her, and she hadn't found any sort of way to fill that gap with the boys in town.

This man? He wasn't from here. He was different.

"Did you ever kill a man?" she asked him.

"That's a personal question to ask a man you just met."

"I think it deserves an answer if you want me to invite you into my home."

His eyes locked with hers. "What if I say yes?"

"Then I'll know you don't back down."

"Does that scare you?" Knox asked her.

Lucy shook her head, "I don't scare easy."

"Good answer."

"Are you coming inside or what?" she asked him.

He got off the bike, went inside her grandad's house, and after that, he never left.

CHAPTER 6

Ruby

Back at the house, Piper Anne and I tell Dodge about the park.

Dodge sits up. "Wait, you couldn't find her?"

"No," I say, "and her phone isn't where her last location was set."

He frowns. "Maybe her phone's just turned off."

"Maybe, but when does a seventeen-year-old girl ever turn off their phone?"

Piper Anne nods, knowing I'm right. "Literally never."

"Exactly," I say. "I'm going to go over to Huck's with Piper Anne. Maybe he will know something more."

"All right," Dodge says. "Keep me posted, and of course, if she shows up here, I'll call right away."

"I love you," I say, pausing before I head back out the door. "But Dodge, even if she lost her phone, it wouldn't have been turned off."

"Maybe it died," Piper Anne says.

"That's true," I say. "Maybe she forgot to charge it last night."

"But why was she at Eagle Crest Park on the last day of school and not with her boyfriend and best friend at the job orientation?" Piper Anne pushes.

"Maple may be secretive, but this is different." Dodge runs a hand over his goatee. "I don't know, Mom, but it doesn't sound good, does it?"

"No," I say. "It really doesn't." I walk over to him and give him a hug and a kiss on the cheek. "I love you. There is food in the fridge. Sorry I can't make you a welcome back from college dinner."

"Don't apologize, Mom. We've got to find Maple, and if we really think she's missing, then I guess going to a police officer's house is the best thing you could possibly do."

I swallow. "It couldn't be the same as the other missing girls, could it? I mean, Maple couldn't actually be missing, could she?"

Dodge and Piper Anne share a look, the look I saw earlier when they were discussing this in the kitchen, a look that says that's exactly what they think has happened.

I drive the five minutes over to Huck's place, parking on the sidewalk. I watch Piper Anne pull into the driveway and walk into the house.

I walk up to his house, feeling strange to be here without Maple. It's a big place for just two people. He and Piper have always flown solo. Huck's wife died when Piper was just a few years old. And in all the years I've known Huck and Piper, I've never known him to date anybody. It must be lonely in this place all by himself, and I wonder what he'll do in a few years when Piper's gone to college.

My heart tightens, though, thinking about Maple. What will I do now if she's really missing? Will I see her again? I bite back tears by clenching my jaw and refusing to go down that dead end. Instead, I knock on the door.

Huck answers. "Hey," he says. "Come in. Jude just got here too."

I step inside, looking to see if I should take off my shoes or not, but everyone else is wearing theirs. The house is set up like a lot of new homes are. A kitchen with a big great room, a fireplace with a TV over it. There are some boxes of takeout on the counter. Pizza and a two-liter of Coke. "Are you hungry?"

I shake my head. "I can't think about food right now."

Jude is eating a slice of pepperoni and takes another bite when I turn back to Huck.

"So, I followed the location on her phone," I explain, filling him and Jude in on what Piper Anne and I discovered at Eagle Creek. "Basically, not much," I finish.

Huck nods. "So, either her phone died, it got turned off, or was destroyed."

"Destroyed?" I cross my arms. "Come on, let's not get dramatic."

His eyes meet mine though, and he tilts his head ever so slightly. "I think it might be time to get dramatic, Ruby."

"Really?" I ask. "I mean, she's probably just—"

"Just what?" Piper says. "Maple doesn't hang out with anybody but me, and Jude sometimes, when she gives him the time of day."

"Ouch," Jude says.

"It's the truth," Piper says.

"You sure there aren't other friends she may be with?" I ask.

"None at the high school at least. She's quiet. She's a loner. She sticks with me."

"And you, do you have other friends?" I ask Piper.

"Sure. I mean, some of the people from art club, and I've been volunteering at the library this year. Dad says it'll probably be good for college applications."

I nod. "Good thinking."

"I like it, too, because I love to read. You know that."

"I do know that," I say smiling. She's the kind of kid who, every year for Christmas, gives her dad a long list of the books she wants for her to-be-read pile. It's endearing. "So, there's nowhere else we can think that she might be?"

39

Jude bites his bottom lip. "I don't know anywhere else," he says, "which makes me feel kind of lame, like maybe I didn't know her as well as I thought I did."

"Don't do that," Piper says. "You knew Maple as much as she'd let you, as much as she'd let anybody."

I swallow. "So, maybe her giving me the cold shoulder lately isn't personal?"

Huck scoffs. "Of course not. She's a teenager."

"Hey," Piper Anne says. "I take offense to that." Piper Anne is so cheery and positive that I can't imagine her ever causing a fight with her dad, but of course, we only know what we see, and I've never seen them behind closed doors. Maybe they have their own fights, their own battles. Just being shut out of your child's life is such a difficult one to swallow. The idea that your kid doesn't want to know you, doesn't want you to know them, feels like a gut punch you can never see coming.

Not after you spent nine months with them in your belly, when you birthed them into the world, imagining a relationship that was deep and true forever. When you are pregnant, you never think when your kid becomes a teenager, they won't want to give you the time of day.

And yes, of course, we all know that that's typical teenage behavior, but every mom, every parent thinks they're going to beat the odds.

And then they don't.

"Hey, did we lose you? I know it's been a long day, why don't you sit down," Huck tries.

I shake my head, pressing my fingertips to my eyes. "No, actually I think I'm not okay. I think I'm actually really scared. What if something actually happened to her? What if she's like Lochlan and Brittany and—"

"Hey," Huck says. "I already made a report at the police station, okay? I'm going to go over there right now and update them with this new information. I think you should come with me, Ruby."

40

"You think?" Going to the police station makes this feel so much more real, like my daughter is really missing.

"She's been missing since eight this morning," Huck says. "It's six o'clock now. If it was an isolated incident, maybe I'd wait. If two other girls from her high school hadn't gone missing just last week, maybe we would give it time, but I think anyone at the station would agree that the third girl gone missing from Eagle High in a week is three too many."

I am relieved that he is making this decision. In my lifetime, I have done my best to avoid the police for the last sixteen years — it is triggering, just the thought of walking into a police station. Of course, Huck has no idea about this. About me.

"Piper Anne, Jude, you guys hang tight, all right? Eat some pizza," Huck directs us all and I appreciate it. I am close to shaking, the fear of it all too much. He takes one look at me and then adds, "Ruby, grab a slice. I have a feeling it's going to be a long night."

The way he says it is ominous. There's no hope there. There's no reason to believe my situation's going to be different than Lochlan or Brittany's, and that makes my stomach turn. Piper must see this because she hands me a glass of water and begins plating me up a slice of pepperoni. "Here," she says. "Eat."

41

CHAPTER 7

Jude

I didn't want to leave Piper's house. Driving back to my dad's place practically killed me, but I knew it would be weird to stay there any longer than I already had been. Ruby's mom had left with Huck, both heading to the police station. Sitting with Piper on the couch felt weird after eleven o'clock at night. She probably wanted to go to bed or something, and not keep hanging out with her best friend's sort of boyfriend.

Piper's dad, Huck, ordered us pizza and got us Coke and it was the most normal kind of thing that I'm guessing Piper just keeps him for granted, a dad who's doing his best to be around, and not just give her a hard time. And Maple's mom was pretty cool. I thought she might judge me or something. Teachers do. You know, because I look kind of like a mess, but all she did was smile, appreciate me being there and speaking up. It's like she was glad to meet me or something. I don't know why Maple is always making comments about how lame her mom is because, not to say Maple is wrong, but Ruby seemed pretty cool.

When I get in the apartment, Dad is on the couch. I try to veer off to my bedroom the moment I enter the front door, but he sees me first.

"Where have you been?" he asks. "You've been gone all day."

There are empty beer cans on the coffee table. He's smoking a cigarette and there's an ashtray that needs to be emptied. I can tell he had a frozen burrito because the wrapper is still on the kitchen counter. I take all this in in a few seconds. My dad flicks his cigarette.

"I was looking for my girlfriend."

He chuckles. "You and that girl Maple, you're a thing now? She's a pretty girl."

"Can you not talk about her?" I ask him. I set down my backpack and kick off my sneakers. I'm not hungry, but I go to the fridge anyways. There's off-brand Coke and I grab a can, popping it open. I lean in the doorway of the kitchen facing my dad who's sitting in the dining room slash living room. We don't have a kitchen table so I don't pull up a seat.

"And yeah, she's kind of my girlfriend, but can you not make comments about her, Dad?" I am not sure how much I want to go into things with him. Do I want to tell him she is missing?

"I'm not saying anything about her. She just looks outta your league. I'm surprised she'd go out with a guy like you."

"Why is that?" I ask.

He chuckles. "I don't know. She's a woman."

"Dad, seriously. Don't talk like that. It's freaky."

He laughs harder, turning down the volume of the TV. "Dude, I'm just messing around. Take a joke."

"It's not funny. And I wasn't just being an ass not coming home earlier. Things are actually kinda serious right now. Maple is missing."

My dad's eyes raise. "Oh yeah? Tell me about it. Let me guess, she ghosted you after you tried to make a move." The way he says it creeps me out like he knows something or he's in on a joke or like it's funny.

I raise my eyebrows, disgusted by this man. "Dad, it's not anything to make light of. She's been missing since like nine o'clock this morning. The last anybody saw her, she was leaving campus, going with some guy, but nobody knows who."

My dad looks away, opens another can of beer, drinks half of it before setting it down. "Well, she probably is having a good time. Can't blame her. The alternative is hanging out with you."

"Seriously, Dad. Stop it." I walk past him through the living room, and grab my backpack.

"Dude, I was just making a joke," he calls after me. "You need to chill out, man. You're never going to get laid this way."

I turn to him. "Don't talk about me like that. You know nothing about me."

He laughs hard slapping his knee. "Oh, so you have been getting laid?"

"I'm not doing this," I say. "And I mean it, stop being weird about Maple. I'm worried about her. I don't know where she is. And two other girls have gone missing last week from school. I'm scared she's mixed up in it, Dad, so please just . . ."

"Oh, I read about that," Dad says, looking at me, slowly giving me a nod. "About the missing girls. I've seen 'em around town. Didn't know they were underage. Used to come to the pool hall."

"You've met them?" I ask, uncomfortable with the idea that my dad is hanging out with girls from school.

"Brittany and Lochlan? Sure, they come out, using fake IDs to drink hard seltzers and shoot the shit." He shrugs. "They're pretty, like Maple."

I want to throw something at him, scream at him, walk out of the apartment and slam the door. But I have nowhere to go and I'm not going to fight with a man who's stronger than me. I've made that mistake enough times in my life. I walk away and head into my bedroom. I set my can of soda on my desk next to my sketchbooks and colored pencils.

I flip through the drawing pad quickly, landing on a sketch of Maple. Seeing the curve of her neck makes my heart feel tight in ways it's never felt before. I know she's beautiful. My dad's not wrong about that, even if he is a creep, but there's something about her that makes me feel like I want to

44

protect her. I've never had that feeling about anyone before in life, like maybe I could do something to make them feel safe.

What good would that feeling get me, though? She's missing and I'm here.

My phone buzzes and I have this moment of hope thinking maybe it's her. I look at the screen.

It's a text from Piper. *You get home okay?*

Yeah, I text back. *The walk's pretty short. It's dark though. Is your dad home yet?*

No. He's probably going to be working all night looking for Maple. I feel weird like we're not doing anything to help.

I think about her words before typing a message back. *What can we do right now though?*

She answers right away. *Maybe we should post about it online?*

I pause before replying. *I don't really have socials,* I finally type out.

Yeah, me either. And I don't hang out with anyone outside of school. She sends a laughing face emoji.

I twist my lips. *She's going to be here tomorrow. She probably wanted some time to be alone. That's all. But, the thing is, she seemed excited to hang out tonight at my house and watch a movie. It was like a whole plan since my dad said we couldn't go to the bonfire.*

Do you wish you would've? I ask her.

Gone to the bonfire tonight? No, especially with Maple gone. It scares me.

My heart feels tight for Piper too. *I don't want you to feel scared. I don't feel scared when I'm talking to you.*

Piper, I text, then I delete. I'm not sure what to say. It almost feels like she is flirting with me, but I don't want to assume that. Assume the worst. Not in a moment like this. *Want to meet up in the morning?* I finally land on those words. They seem safe enough, and I do want to be around Piper Anne. She's the closest thing I have to Maple right now.

Of course, she types back. *Let's meet for coffee at Coffee Planet. At eight? Before we go work at the club at ten?*

Sounds good, I reply. *I hope you can get some sleep.*

She replies, *If my dad texts anything with an update, I'll let you know. Okay?*

I lay down on my bed with my phone against my chest, wishing there was more I could do in this moment, wondering why my dad has to give me a hard time, all the time.

I wonder what my dad was doing today . . . if he was working.

For some reason, I'm too nervous to ask. The answer might scare me. It might tell me something I'm not ready to hear.

But I don't think I will be able to sleep tonight so long as this thought is running through my mind.

CHAPTER 8

Ruby

Driving home from the police station is painful. The passenger side seat is unbearably empty. It's times like this I wish I had a partner, a person, someone who had my back, who was in my corner. Who would look at me and say, "Ruby, you got this. You're not alone."

It's times like this I wish I had Grandpa. I wish I had his microwave TV dinner and Wheel of Fortune. His La-Z-Boy recliner and the couch right next to it that I would curl up on while he listened to Vanna White. It's times like this I wish I had someone who knew me from before, who'd known me since forever, but I don't have that person. And right now I don't even have Maple.

When I pull up to the house, I tell myself to keep it together. Huck told me that right now, I need to stay strong. And I know he is right, that is what Dodge needs right now. I may not have a life partner, but I am Dodge's mom and he needs me to show up as a beacon of courage.

Having Huck at my side at the police station was a good thing.

Once we arrived at the station, Officer Rodgers immediately introduced himself as the detective assigned to assist with the case. He is a tall, lean man with thinning hair, in his early sixties. He talked me through the process, and I kept looking between him and Huck, wanting to be sure these men were on the same page. At one point Huck looked at me and nodded, "You can trust him, Ruby. I promise."

I don't have anything against cops, but the memories I associate with them are so strong, it is difficult to remain present even as Rodgers is asking me to describe Maple so he can enter her information into the National Crime Information Center Missing Persons File. Apparently, if you are under eighteen there is no waiting period before they will input a child's information.

I told them all I could. She is 5'6", 150 pounds, curly hair. That she always wore an amber necklace, the one I gave her for her thirteenth birthday. She wears rings stacked on every finger. I don't tell them that when she was little I called her my witch baby because just looking at her felt like she was casting a spell. She was secretive then too, like she had tapped into her shadow side years before most people do. Did she become this way because of the pain I carried when she entered the world? Has she always felt dark because she was born into a world with little light?

I would place candles on her birthday cake every year and when she closed her eyes to make a wish it was always like she was making a promise.

God, how I wish I knew what she dreamed would come true.

Does she want to be missing? Did she leave on purpose? Or was my little girl taken?

I will be haunted by this until she is found.

They had me call Dodge immediately and tell him not to let anyone inside or home. "Do not touch or remove anything from your child's room," Officer Rodgers instructed. "Tomorrow I will come out with a team and do a thorough search. There may be clues found on her clothes or in her personal items."

Rodgers also put out a Be On The Lookout Bulletin, which would ensure all officers in the area were alerted to the fact a third girl in Eagle Crest was missing.

"When I come tomorrow, I am going to want a list of any family, friends or acquaintances that Maple might know or speak with. We are also going to want a recent photograph to help with the search."

I nodded, sitting in that sterile space, wanting to remember everything.

"Don't worry," Huck assured me. "You won't be alone in this."

And I am grateful, of course, to have him with me. Still, as I get out of my car, and walk to the house, I am distinctly aware that he's not my person, that I don't have a person and never have. I have been going through life on my own ever since I lost Grandad.

Huck is a good man, but he's helping because he is Piper's dad, and is simply doing his job.

Do I wish he would be more than that? I'm not quite sure.

And it's not even the time to wonder. Right now, it feels like the time to pray, to look for one of those miracles I'm always wanting to find.

When I pull up to my house I'm surprised to see Tom and Nora's car there. I walk in through the back kitchen door and find them washing dishes.

"Oh, you're home," Nora says, setting down a dish towel and coming over to give me a hug. It is a comfort to see my best friend here. "Any news?" she asks.

I shake my head. "Nothing really."

"Well, we came over with some food, put some take out in the fridge and freezer," Tom says. "And we got you some pastries for the morning," Nora adds. "I know it's not much, but we didn't know what we can do to help."

49

"Thank you both so much," I say, grateful for their care. "I'm just gonna go say hi to Dodge, okay?"

"Of course. We are just gonna finish this load and then get out of your hair so you can rest," Nora says.

When I walk down the hall into the living room I find Dodge watching a show. "Everything here okay?" I ask.

He pauses the show immediately, not actually interested in the show. He wants to know where Maple is.

"It's nothing different than when I called you from the station. No word from her, and no one has reported seeing her," I say, shaking my head, feeling like the entire day has been a cruel joke.

"Shit, Mom, really?"

At this, seeing him reminds me that there actually has been someone with me for a really long time.

Dodge has been with me since the very beginning. Without him, I wouldn't have had the strength to survive at all. I owe my son my life.

The tears begin to fall. Tears I've held back for hours. And I don't want to burden Dodge, especially not now, but right now I can't help it. "Huck was with me at the station and got a preliminary report started, and they will be here tomorrow to work on the investigation."

"Good," Dodge says, sitting up, resting his arms on his knees, listening intently.

"It seems like it's going to be all hands on deck since there are two girls who have gone missing already."

"They think it might really be linked?"

"It's looking like that, 'isn't it? Three girls from the same school, the same age." I shake my head. I kick off my clogs and sit down on the couch next to Dodge.

"Do you want any dinner?" he asks. "Nora and Tom brought Thai food."

"No, I had a slice of pizza at Huck's."

"It's kind of serendipitous that Maple's best friend's dad is a cop, isn't it?" he says.

I nod. Maybe that's a miracle. Maybe there are miracles everywhere.

I exhale, "I feel like I should be doing something, going somewhere, looking for her. Instead, I'm just . . ." I shake my head.

"Where would you go, Mom? Where are you going to call?"

"You're right," I say, "That's the problem. I think I knew Maple even less than I thought. I didn't know she had a boyfriend."

"He seems nice, right?" Dodge asks.

"Yeah, a little scruffy. Kind of like a stray dog. And I mean that in the sweetest way possible."

Dodge laughs. "Do you want some tea or something?"

I look at him. "You are being very sweet, Dodge. What would I do without you?"

He shrugs. "I don't know. But you are the only mom I've got, I'm the only son you have. We've gotta look out for one another, right?" He smiles and he looks like the little boy I remembered earlier, the one who played in the pool at the base of the waterfall, smiling like summer. Smiling like true freedom.

I may have messed a lot of things up, but I didn't mess that up. I got my kids out of there alive.

"I want something stronger than tea," I say, standing up from the couch and walking toward the dining room that is adjacent to the kitchen. Dodge turns the movie back on as I walk over to the sideboard in the dining room, one that looks as much like the one in the old farmhouse as I could possibly hunt down from an antique shop. From here I can see Nora and Tom. They stopped washing dishes and are speaking in low voices. I reach for a glass tumbler, and pour myself an inch of whiskey. I take a sip, listening from the dark dining room.

"That's the thing, Tom," Nora says. "I think Ruby isn't quite sure what Maple's like these days. She keeps her cards close."

"So what did Huck have to say?"

51

"He is taking it seriously. I guess they were pushing it up the chain because of those other two missing girls."

Tom sighs. "Damn. I really hope that's not the case."

"I know," Nora says. I see her reach for Tom's hand, squeezing it. I don't want to eavesdrop, but I don't want to interrupt. These two have been married for sixteen years. Somehow seeing Tom embrace my best friend gives me a jolt of hope, that there still is love in the world.

When Nora pulls back and looks into Tom's eyes, I don't expect the words that come out of her mouth in little more than a whisper. "It makes me wonder about Ruby's life, like what's actually going on."

"What do you mean?" he asks.

"We've been together forever and there's no mysteries between us, but we've been friends with Ruby for so long and there's still so many unknowns about her."

Tom frowns. "What are you getting at?"

"Don't you think it's weird how we know nothing about her past? I don't even know where she lived before Eagle Crest."

Tom looks at Nora. "I don't know if we should be poking around in your best friend's life. It seems like it could get messy. It seems like you could lose her."

"I'm not saying anything. I don't really know what I'm saying or even thinking. It's just her kids are maybe a mess right now, and well, like it's genetic or something?" Nora shrugs.

"Is it? I don't know," Tom says.

"Well, you're the pediatrician. You should know about child development."

"Well, genetics are real, of course. Alcoholism is passed down. All sorts of tendencies are. But Ruby is stable. In all the time we've known her she's never gone off the deep end."

"That's true," Nora says. "She is steady, and she really made a life for herself. Like that was gumption. Remember when she was sending that manuscript around to all those agents, trying to get a book deal? She had tenacity."

Tom nods. "I agree. I don't think you need to be worried about Ruby. So maybe she has a past that's less than desirable, but maybe she has her reasons for keeping a secret. We're not talking about it. Maybe it's self-preservation."

"Maybe people keep secrets though because they need to' hide something," Nora presses.

"What would Ruby be hiding? Sure, she got pregnant when she was young, had two kids back-to-back and doesn't want to talk about their dad. But that isn't some dark secret, Nora."

"The kids don't know who their father is," Nora says.

"Well, maybe that's for the best. Maybe Ruby is protecting them."

"Are you curious?"

"Honestly, no. I have enough to worry about in my own life." The conversation seems to have come to a natural end and I realize I drank all the whiskey without even thinking. I set down the empty tumbler, the words of Nora and Tom rolling in my head.

They aren't wrong. I never have opened up about my past. Now, it seems too late. I walk back to Dodge in the living room, and Nora and Tom join us.

"Dishes are done," Nora says. "Do you promise to call tomorrow as soon as you know more?"

I nod, yawning as I do. "I really hope this is all a misunderstanding. That she is home in the morning."

"We do too," Tom says, giving me a hug. "We love you guys."

"I'm exhausted," I say. "I'm going to take a hot shower and hope that tomorrow morning something happens. Something like Maple coming home."

I tell them all goodnight before heading up the stairs. The shower is steaming hot, just like I'd hoped. I wash my face and brush my teeth, wondering where my daughter is right now. How she is. If she's freezing cold, if she's hurt, if she's been left for dead. Those words seem so insane, yet it's what's running through my mind as I crawl into bed. I toss and turn all night, thinking of the past, wishing I could rewind so much.

Knowing that is simply impossible. Knowing all I can do right now is hope for a miracle.

* * *

I wake in the morning, grateful I got a few hours of sleep at least. The fact I got any sleep at all makes me feel a little sick inside, like something's wrong with me. Why could I sleep in the middle of this? Shouldn't I be wracked all night? Instead, those hours I was asleep, I slept hard, like my body knew I needed to escape the truth.

As I'm making a pot of coffee there's a knock on the back door that surprises me. There is still no noise coming from Dodge's bedroom and I assume he is still asleep. I look through the window on the door, and I see that it's Jude.

"Hey," I say in surprise as I pull open the door. Maybe he has news. My heart buoys. "It's only six in the morning. What's up? Did you hear from her? Did you hear from Maple?"

He shakes his head. "No, sorry. I wish I had, I wish I knew something, but . . ."

"What? Do you want some coffee?"

"I'm meeting Piper in a couple hours for coffee. I don't know. I couldn't sleep. I tried to. I just kept walking around all night."

"You've been up all night?" I ask.

He shrugs. I look at him more closely. His eyes are bloodshot. He's in the same clothes as yesterday, except for he has a hoodie thrown over his shirt. "What's on your mind?"

I pour him some coffee and add half-and-half and shove the bowl of sugar toward him. He adds two spoonfuls before taking a sip.

I feel like I want to take this boy under my wing, make him a stack of pancakes, bacon and eggs. It looks like he hasn't had a home-cooked meal in a while.

"Look," he says as we both sit down at the kitchen table. "Maybe it's nothing. Maybe I'm just losing my mind, but . . ."

"Just say it, Jude. What are you thinking?"

"The thing is my dad . . ."

I frown. "What about your dad?"

I take a sip from my coffee. Completely unsure where this is going, but wanting to understand.

"I'm not trying to start something and maybe it's nothing, but my dad made comments to Maple when they met."

The hairs on the back of my neck stand up. "Maple met your dad?"

He nods, "Yeah, she came over a few times and he was there."

"Right," I say slowly, wondering when those times might have been. After school or at night when she said she's out with Piper and I believed her.

I'm always at home. It's where I work. Why did she cut me out so intensely? Why didn't she want me to have any part of her life? I swallow. "All right. Your dad met her and what was that like?"

"He just said how pretty she was, like to her. He was like, "You look so good. You should wear shorter skirts." Or like, "You don't have to wear a baggy T-shirt, you know." Shit like that."

My eyes widen in surprise. I've known men like this, and worse, but I hate that my daughter was in contact with someone like that. "Yeah. It is really inappropriate."

"Yeah, that's why I told her I didn't like her coming around, but she said she didn't mind. She thought it was funny. But did she think it was funny or was she just saying she thought it was funny to not make it weird?"

I exhale, "Honestly, Jude, I don't know. I've never met your dad. I've never seen Maple around him."

"The thing is tonight, when I told him she was gone, he kind of looked away like he wouldn't meet my eyes. And then I made a comment about the other girls who went missing and it seemed like . . ."

I frown. "Did your dad know those other girls?"

"He knew them. Met them at the pool hall, I guess. Hung out with them there."

I look at Jude. I don't know this boy well enough to know whether or not he's completely fabricating this story or if it's absolutely true, but at this moment I have nothing else to go on.

"I'm not trying to assume the worst," he continues. "That's why I was walking around all night. I was thinking about it. I met you and you're a good mom. And you love Maple. And maybe I'm a shitty son, but all I know is this. If my dad happened to have any information on where she might be, we should try to find that out. Right?"

"Jude, can you come with me to the police station? Anything they could use as a lead is worth looking into."

He nods. "My dad's going to kill me."

"Can you live with that?"

He nods. "For Maple? Yeah. Feels like for Maple, I'd do anything."

BLAMELESS BUT BROKEN
by Ruby Clarke

CHAPTER 5

Lucy had never been in love. Not properly, not romantically, and Knox seemed to know that intrinsically. He knew what to do to make her feel wanted, seen, heard. And it worked, for a while at least. But eventually the shine wore off and instead of dates to the drive-in, flowers on Friday, and motorcycle rides to Fish Hook Lake, he would ask where she'd been.

"I was just working at the diner," she'd tell him, honestly, pulling out cash from her pockets. "Look, I made sixty-eight bucks tonight in tips."

He wasn't impressed. Other times, she'd go to the grocery store or the library on a Saturday, pinching pennies because even though she was working full-time at the diner and the house was paid off, she had a car payment and gas, the phone bill, electricity, and she was trying to save.

"What are you hoarding your money away for anyways?" Knox would ask her.

There was always an edge to it too, a judgment. He'd only known her six weeks, but sometimes it felt like it'd been six years. Like he had a right to know things about her she had never shared with anybody, like how she was saving up this money because one day she was going to go to college and when she went to college, she was going to study art history.

She didn't know much about art but she would pore over pages in those big books with glossy pictures. Absorbing them. She went to a museum in New York City once, on a school field trip, overnight, and she fell in love. She came home and checked out art history books at the library. She poured over the pages imagining what it would be like to go back to the Met one day.

She would imagine what it would be like to go to Paris and see Monet's lilies or go to Egypt and see Cleopatra's museum. In the old farmhouse the only art on the walls were her grandma's paint-by-numbers, which were special in their own way, just a different way than the masterpieces she read about.

She didn't want to say that to him because he might not understand. Because why did she care about art anyways? Well, he'd have to know her to know that, and the reason she cared about art was because she'd heard that's what her grandma loved the most. And sometimes just having one detail like that, about someone you never even met, was enough to make it feel like you knew them by heart.

Lucy didn't tell Knox about her plans for her life. She was still so young. Twenty-one and unsure of where things might go with Knox. And even though she liked him, nearly loved him, she also knew there were a lot of questions she didn't have answers to. And while he was busy grilling her about where she was when she was buying apples and oranges for the week, she had no idea where he was.

"What'd you do all day?" she'd ask, after pulling a ten-hour shift at the diner, her feet aching, her calves tight.

All she wanted to do was put up her feet on the couch and have him sit down and massage them. He did the first few weeks they were together, he would kiss her pinky toes and tease her about how her feet smelled, and she'd laugh, throwing a pillow at him. And they would make something for dinner. Spaghetti and meatballs or taco salad. They felt like a couple. Not that she had much experience of what those were like. Knox didn't either.

It was still summer then, fireflies out and a moon milky and full, and she wanted to stay in this feeling of falling in love. She wanted to capture that feeling and hold it in her tummy because a part of her knew, even at the start, that this thing had a shelf life. Knox wasn't the kind of man who would stay.

But God, she still would close her eyes and make a wish, hoping that they could beat the odds.

"Were your parents married?" she'd ask, sitting on the front porch with a bowl of pasta in her lap.

He'd shake his head. "I mean, I told you about them. Nothing good came from my family."

Lucy would sigh, feeling like she wasn't going to get much more than that from him on that topic.

"Not much good came from mine either. And I can really only remember one of them anyways. The rest are just memories from stories that might not even be true."

He'd tuck a strand of hair behind her ear, look at her adoringly. "Except you came from them. Seem like pretty good stock in my books."

Words like that would make her heart swell. Make her think that the foot rubs weren't necessary. That standing in the kitchen together, rolling little balls of ground beef mixed with onion powder and bread crumbs and browning them on the stove top wasn't necessary. That words were enough.

But even with all her hoping and wishing, Lucy learned pretty quickly that words were not enough. Not even a little, not even at all.

"I told you I was trying to look for work," Knox would tell her when she'd ask what he was doing while she was working a double. The laundry wasn't washed. Food wasn't made. The grass was getting longer by the day.

59

"Did you have any luck? What kind of work are you looking for?" She would tiptoe around what she really wanted to ask: Are you looking for work? And, if you aren't, can you please help out around the house a little bit?

Not to mention the other questions that were brewing. Questions like how are you making any money at all? How are you paying for the gas in your motorcycle? And sometimes she'd come home and there would be a case of beer in the fridge. She hadn't paid for it. He had money coming from somewhere, something. Not to mention they'd go out every once in a while, grab hamburgers after taking a ride on the motorcycle, or popcorn at the movie theater. He'd pay for that. She wanted to know where he'd been going before he stopped at the diner and found her.

But he didn't like those questions. He didn't like any questions at all, unless he was the one thinking of them. Unless he was the one asking.

"I was looking for work downtown," he'd say, the least helpful answer possible.

Downtown had lots of businesses. There was a hardware store and a mechanic shop. She had no idea if he was capable of working at either of those places. She knew virtually nothing about his past. All she knew was when they were together that sometimes she forgot about everything she didn't have. And while at first that seemed like enough, she was growing awfully aware of how little that mattered when she was pinching pennies to make life work.

"You know, one of my customers, Dylan Kenny, he has a construction business," she would say, trying to be helpful. "He's always looking for day workers."

Knox would scoff, cracking open a beer. "I don't need no day work."

"Right," she'd say slowly, choosing her words with care. "So what kind of work are you looking for?"

"To be honest, I'd rather be in the moment," he'd say, reaching for her waist, patting her bottom, making her blush and feel like a fool all at the same time.

Why was it so easy for her to cave? Is it part of some people's DNA? The ability to look past red flags when they got desperate enough?

Knox was still talking, "Do we have to talk about work all the time? Can't we just talk about the present? You, me, looking for a movie to watch? Microwaving some popcorn?"

"Sure," she'd say. "Let me take a quick shower and then I'll meet you on the couch."

But when she'd get back on the couch in sweatpants and a hoodie, freshly showered, he had gone off on the motorcycle. She'd wait up, knowing he'd get home eventually, all the while she had the resounding sensation that this was literally what it meant to be wasting one's life away.

Knox would return a few hours later obviously drunk, eyes bloodshot.

"Where have you been?" she'd ask, hating the question. That she even cared.

She'd known this man, what? Six weeks? Did he owe her all the information? But then again, he was sleeping in her grandad's house, sleeping in a bed with her. Not that they were doing much sleeping. They were having plenty of fun doing other things. Other things that kept her distracted from the warning signs that were all around Knox, and that was before she found out the truth.

One day she was working the diner and Carl came in.

Carl was a regular. He was maybe five, six years older than her, but she'd grown up around him. Knew his family lived in the trailer at the edge of town. Had no reason not to trust him, but she admitted that today he was looking a lot worse for wear.

"Your man around here?" Carl asked her.

"You mean Knox?" She had never heard someone refer to him as hers.

"Yeah. Your fella. He around here?"

"I don't know where he is," she said honestly. When she had left for work at the diner this morning he was still passed out in bed.

"Well, I looked for him at your grandad's house, he wasn't there. And he wasn't at Gunnison Ave like he promised."

She frowned, the only thing on that street was a pawn shop. "What was he doing on Gunnison?"

Carl looked at her with a squint in his eyes as if testing her. "You know what he's doing," he said.

But she didn't. She had no idea whatsoever.

Carl left, eyes red and twitching, as if he was looking for a fix. She knew that. And that's when she wondered if she'd asked Knox any of the right questions.

That first night they met, she'd asked him if he had ever killed anybody. And while he didn't answer it directly, she was thinking maybe the other question she should have asked was if he was dealing drugs.

It took her a bit to put things together, but now she was having a sinking suspicion that's exactly what Knox had been up to.

62

CHAPTER 9

Ruby

Jude gets in my car, and I call Huck before getting into the driver's side.

"Hey," I say, after he answers right away. "Can I come over real quick? I have Jude here and he seems to think his father might be involved somehow."

"Seriously? Damn, of course, come over, I haven't left for the station yet."

When Jude and I pull up to their house, he speaks up. "Look, can we not talk about my dad around Piper Anne? I don't want . . ."

"Jude, of course, I would never put you in a position that would make you uncomfortable. If you'd rather we go straight to Detective Rodgers, we can do that too."

He shakes his head. "No this is fine, I trust Huck."

As if on cue, Huck opens the front door. "Morning, you hungry, Jude?"

He shrugs. "I could eat."

Inside the house the smell of pancakes greets us. Piper Anne is sitting on a stool with a stack covered in syrup with a side of sausage links.

63

"So," she says, chewing a bite. "On a scale of one to ten, regarding my level of freakout, I would say I'm pretty much at a ten. It's worst-case everything. I mean even Dad's scared. I can tell he is and he doesn't usually get freaked out. He's usually cool, calm, and collected. But last night, I saw that look in his eye, a look that said, 'This is bad'."

"It is bad," Huck says, handing Jude a plate of food who slides in next to Piper Anne and begins eating. "But we are going to find her. And every little bit helps."

"Dad didn't even come home until after one in the morning. He'd been at the station trying to make a plan, but there is no plan." Her shoulders fall and she begins to cry. Hucks eyes widen and he reaches around Piper Anne's shoulders, squeezing them.

"Look, everyone's worried," he says. "That's the most I can say because we don't know anything else right now. We have nothing to go on yet. But Detective Rodgers has been assigned to the case and they'll start investigating today. They will go to Ruby's house and check out Maple's room, interview people, that sort of thing."

"Will they interview me?" Piper Anne asks.

"Of course," Huck says. "You're her best friend. You know her better than anyone. That's why I'm telling you, sweetheart. If there's something you're not saying, if there's anything you know . . ."

"I don't. I'm not holding anything back. I promise. I would tell you if I was."

"You swear?"

Huck looks at his daughter like she is hiding something.

"I'm not hiding anything at all. In fact, I'm telling the whole truth as I know it. The main problem is I don't know *much* truth. In fact, I don't know much of anything."

"I have work today . . . should I go? My shift starts at ten."

"Mine does too," Jude says.

"But you are going to talk with Huck first, right?" I ask.

Jude nods. Piper Anne frowns. "Why does Jude have to talk to my dad?"

Jude's jaw tenses. "I'll tell you later," he says, shoveling the rest of the food in his mouth.

"Wait, did you think of something over the night, something that could help us, help us find Maple? Because no matter how many times I run it through in my mind, I can't think of anything that could even be remotely helpful. I have no idea where she was and that makes me feel like a terrible best friend. Shouldn't I know where she is?"

"Piper Anne, you are being too hard on yourself," I say. "If someone kidnapped Maple, there is nothing you could have done."

"And even if she ran away on her own accord, you are not responsible for her actions," Huck adds.

"But shouldn't I have some idea of who she left school with? And what kind of friend is she anyways if she wouldn't even tell me something basic like that? Did she care for me at all?"

"I think we all know Maple cared a great deal for you," I say. I begin wondering why I wanted to come here in the first place, maybe I should have taken straight to the police station, or called Officer Rodgers and had him come to me.

I feel all over the place, like I am making rash decisions without thinking through the implications.

"Look," I say, feeling like Piper Anne is still mid-meltdown. And I don't blame her for having one, but I don't think Jude and I need to witness it. "I think Jude and I ought to go to the station and meet you there later, Huck."

"But wait," Piper Anne adds, tears falling down her face. "What if I am an even more terrible friend to assume the worst and start making this about me. Maybe she was just walking to get a coffee, and someone forced her into a white van, never to return?"

"I know not knowing is torture," Jude says. "We all just want her home, safe."

"I don't think you two can work today," Huck says, making an executive decision. "I will call the club myself and let them know the extenuating circumstances, okay?"

"So, wait, why are you all going to the police station without me?" Piper Anne asks.

I look at Jude. "Maybe you go with Huck and I take Piper Anne home with me."

Piper Anne looks at Jude, questioningly. "Why did you have to go to the police station?"

He runs a hand over his jaw before taking a bite of sausage. "You sure you won't say anything?"

"I promise," she says, setting down her fork and looking at him with intensity.

I look at Huck, wondering if this is appropriate, but he doesn't stop Jude, so neither do I.

"It might be nothing. And I don't know what kind of piece of shit son I am for even suggesting this, but . . ." he looks at Piper Anne, "I can trust you, right?"

"Totally. Scout's honor."

He gives her a wry smile. "I guess your dad's a cop and you're Maple's best friend. And her mom already knows, so."

"Just out with it," Piper Anne says. "You're freaking me out."

"I'm really hoping it's nothing, but I just wanted the cops to know that I think my dad might be involved."

"Involved in what?" Piper Anne asks.

He shrugs, looking past her. "Involved in something about the missing girls."

"About Maple and . . ."

"Yeah, all of them. There's just something about my dad that seems off when he was around Maple, the way he looked at her, his unaccounted time. I don't really know what he's doing for work these days. And he'll come and he'll go and I don't know, Piper. I think he might be doing something sketch."

My whole body seems to tense as I hear him lay it out loud. I have no idea if Jude is jumping to conclusions. But from my experience it is better to ask more questions, not fewer.

66

Jude continues, "I figure they can look into my dad without tracing it back to me. My dad won't know. And maybe it has nothing to do with him at all, and my dad's just a pervert who likes to hit on teenagers but . . ."

"Oh my gosh," Piper Anne says, covering her mouth. "Jude, you are being really brave."

I want to reach out and squeeze his hand. I want to give him a hug. I feel a tenderness for him as he speaks. There's a rawness to his voice, to his words. He has a tenderness to his soul that I hear when he speaks.

"I'm hoping you're wrong," I say.

He nods. "Me too. But unless we get more information, it's the only thing I have to work on right now."

"I wish we could get on her phone," Piper Anne says.

Jude sets down his fork. "How come?"

"She used Snapchat all the time. Maybe we could log into her account and find out who she was talking to."

Jude frowns. "That's probably illegal. Besides, we don't have her phone."

"I know, but I'm her best friend," Piper Anne says, looking at her dad and I. "I'm pretty sure I could figure out her login. That could be helpful, right?"

Jude pulls out his phone. "Well, I don't have that app on my phone. We could download it and try to get in."

I press my lips together, wondering what they might find, if it could give us the answers we need. Suddenly I am beyond thankful we came here before the police station. It seems these two teenagers may know more about Maple than they seem to believe.

Piper Anne pauses. "What if we find out something we don't like?"

Jude snorts. "I promise you, anything's better than the idea of my own father being the person who kidnapped my girlfriend." He hands Piper Anne his phone to download the app and try to log in.

And I figure with this level of honesty, Jude is a friend we can trust.

CHAPTER 10

Ruby

The plan is for Huck to bring Jude into the police station. As I drive away from Huck's house, I can't help but consider everything that Jude laid out for me about his father. Questioning his own dad's motives, his reasons for coming to me in the first place. He thinks his dad might be guilty, might be implicated somehow in the missing girls.

The level of unease that must be going on in Jude's home is sickening.

When we were in the car together I had asked him all about his life, how he got to where he is now. He told me about his mom moving out, moving to Arizona with her new husband a few months ago, how that meant he was living with his dad for the first time. How it also means he's getting to know his dad in a whole new light and none of it is good.

Of course, it made me think about my own childhood, the way I was raised, who brought me up in this world, how I never really knew my parents, how my grandad was my whole wide world for so long, and how losing him changed me from the inside out, forced me down a path that changed the trajectory of my whole life. It brought me Dodge and it brought me Maple and it took me away from so much else.

My eyes fill with tears as I drive home, the memories surfacing and it's not the time for it. It really isn't. Right now, I should be focused only on finding Maple, not on my past and what's brought me here. Only about finding my little girl, my baby, my Maple.

As I park at my house, I pull out my phone before walking in the door alone. Piper Anne plans to drive over here after she showers and calms down a bit. I check to see if I've missed any calls or messages, hoping against hope that somehow Maple's left me a message, shared her location, anything, but there's nothing. There's no update from her. I check her location and it's still at the same spot, Eagle Crest Park, like yesterday.

I know she wasn't in those woods, but I have a feeling that's the first place Huck and Detective Rodgers are going to send a crew. It makes sense, it's her last known location and maybe at least with that bit of information, they will be able to track a vehicle, something, anything to bring us closer to her.

As I hold my phone in my hand, it buzzes. I jump, hoping it's Maple. Instead, it's Nora. I answer, feeling like hearing from my best friend is exactly what I need right now.

"Hey," I say, my voice immediately wobbly.

"Oh, babe. You holding up okay?"

"Not really," I admit. "None of this feels real."

"Look, I am just on my way back from the bakery and grabbed some food for you and Dodge. Can I swing by and drop it off?"

"Of course. I'm just crying in my car."

"Hang tight. I'll be there in five."

I close my eyes, not ready to go inside and tell Dodge more upsetting news: namely that there is no news on where his sister might be.

Nora's car pulls up next to mine on the driveway. She is in wide-legged jeans and a plain white tee with high top Vans.

She has a pink pastry box and I get out of my car to meet her, slinging my purse over my shoulder and sliding my phone in my back jeans pocket.

"Morning sweetie," she says, giving me a half-hug and handing me the box. "Any update?"

"The officer assigned to the case is coming over soon. I think they are going to go through Maple's room, look for clues. It's all a nightmare, Nora."

"I know. I wish there was something I could do."

"I think they are starting search parties this morning too."

"I will be there," she says.

I pause, feeling unsettled about what I briefly overhead in my kitchen last night. "I'm not trying to be intense, but I heard you and Tom in my kitchen last night."

Nora's eyes meet mine. "We're worried."

"You think I'm hiding something?" I bite my bottom lip.

Nora sighs. "I know you are. And that is okay, I just want you to know I love you, no matter what happened in the past."

"I can't do this right now, Nora. It's too much."

"I didn't want to pry, but I was thinking, what if someone from your past came for Maple? I wondered if maybe you have an idea of who could have gone after Maple but you are too scared to say?"

"It's not that," I say, not wanting to go this deep with Nora. I trust her, she is the closest friend I have ever had, but I know I have kept walls up around our relationship. She is just too kind of a person to press.

Tears fill Nora's eyes. "I was up all night worried sick. But also feeling like a terrible friend. I wonder what sort of person doesn't know where her best friend grew up, what your parents are like. If they are even alive. Where you went to high school. I should know those things, Ruby. I should know you."

I wipe the tears falling down my cheeks. Scared to say anything. "You are the best friend I have ever had. You have loved me even though I have kept you and Tom at arm's length. You have always given me the benefit of the doubt. I came here to Eagle Crest, running from my past, you knew that and instead of forcing me to talk you gave me space to heal."

Nora's hand reaches out for mine. "I know, but you came here over a decade ago."

I swallow, knowing in my heart Nora is right, terrified of the idea that my past is linked to my present — to Maple's disappearance.

"Thank you for bringing these pastries," I say. "And I'm not trying to brush what you've said under the rug. I hear you, Nora. I just can't go there quite yet. Can you be patient with me?"

She nods, giving me another hug. "Tom and I love you, and Dodge, and Maple. We are here for you, no matter what."

As she gets back in her car and drives away, I feel a wave of emotion run over me. There is a sadness in my belly, knowing life could have been so different if I had a friend like her in my life when Grandpa died, someone who would have sat with me as I healed from my loss. Instead, I tried to fix that hole in my heart in so many wrong ways. In ways that broke me.

I wipe my eyes, and turn to the house. When I walk in the door, Dodge is sitting on the couch. "Hey, Mom," he says. "How'd it go at the station?"

I set my purse down in an armchair and hand him the box of treats. "Those are from Nora."

I slide off my sandals as I sit cross-legged in the chair, wanting to fill him in.

He opens the box and pulls out a croissant, taking a bite. "I made another pot of coffee if you want it," he says.

"Thanks," I tell him, "but I'm coffeed out."

It's so odd having a grown child, one who makes pots of coffee without being asked. At least it is for me, and I'm thankful that I've made that transition with Dodge. In so many ways, it's what I've always dreamed of for my children and my relationship with them. To have it now with him makes me long for Maple to be home, to ensure that I have that with her too. It's Dodge's first summer out of college, this is not how I expected his home-coming to go. Tears fill my eyes as I think of it.

"Mom, don't cry, tell me everything. Are you okay?"

"I'm not okay," I say, running a hand over my neck. "I keep thinking about Maple and you, and you guys when you were little, and now you're all grown up and now she's gone and Dodge, I'm nervous about your future, about where Maple might be and—"

"Don't think about me right now," he says.

I shake my head, wiping away a tear. "As if I can *not* think about you. You're my little boy."

"Mom, don't think of me and my childhood right now. The timing isn't right for reminiscing."

"Timing in life never is," I tell him, feeling defeated by the truth of it. "Just get that through your head now, it'll save you a lot of grief over time, over the years. There's never a per-fect moment, never the right situation. I mean, maybe there's going to be the right moment on a Wednesday in the middle of the month at 2.30 a.m. when everyone else in the world's asleep. That's the only moment where you'll have complete peace, where it's going to feel like all the stars have aligned."

He looks at me, "Mom, I thought you believed in miracles. There's got to be more miracles than a random Wednesday at 2 a.m."

"Maybe I've lost hope for miracles."

"What happened at the station?" he asks to get the con-versation back on track.

I tell him about Jude and his worries about his father, that his dad might be somehow connected to the girls missing. "Huck was taking him to the station now."

"Oh shit," Dodge says. "Mom, that's pretty bad."

"I know. It makes you kind of lose hope in humanity, doesn't it?"

"Yeah, it does." He stands, reaching for my hand to pull me up. "Come on, let's go make some eggs or something."

"All right," I say, grateful for the distraction. I can crack some eggs and scramble them up and add cheese and onions and fill a few tortillas. Going through the motions might make this less horrific, all of it. Folding up a burrito instead of thinking about the way my life itself is unraveling.

Just as we finish eating our breakfast burritos, there's a knock on the front door. I go to answer it and see it's Huck and Detective Rodgers.

"Come in," I say. "Did you get a chance to talk with Jude?"

"Yes," Detective Rogers says. "He was very cooperative and we appreciate his help."

Huck speaks up, "He was planning on meeting up with Piper over at the school where the canvassing is starting."

I take in the information. "People are out looking for Maple?"

Huck nods. "They will be breaking out into groups to begin covering ground shortly. You can head over there too, once we finish here."

"Of course I will go help," I say, wishing I could go now, wanting to scour every inch of land until I find my daughter. The three of us sit in the living room, and Officer Rodgers pulls out a legal pad and pen. Dodge joins us and introduces himself. Then Rodgers looks at me.

"I heard from some old friends that they are meeting at the school to look for Maple. I didn't realize everyone already knew she was missing."

Rodgers addresses Dodge. "The school has been notified of the situation and they did a caller this morning, notifying families in the district that another student is missing. Students have been advised not to go out alone. We want to put an end to whatever is happening in Eagle Crest, not multiply it."

It is my worst nightmare — my little girl being a part of this horrific investigation. "What can I do?"

"Well, it is important that we talk with anyone Maple may have been close with, coworkers, neighbors, teachers.

We have to go on what we know about Maple, who she was friends with, what she might've been doing in her free time."

"Piper's her only friend. You should be interviewing her."

"We will be," Huck says, "after we speak with you and we get things moving with the case."

"The case," I repeat, realizing just how serious all of this is. My daughter has been missing for twenty-four hours. There's two other girls who haven't been found in town. I press my fingertips to the bridge of my nose.

"Hey," Dodge says, squeezing my hand, trying to calm me. "We can answer his questions, one at a time. What are the neighbors' names? I know Dot and Robbie are on the right of us."

I nod. "And Tim and Leroy are on the left. She used to babysit for Miranda across the street."

"That is good," Rodgers says. "Any other adults in her life?"

"Nora, of course, and her husband Tom. They have been our closest family friends since the kids were little. She just got hired at the country club to work this summer, but I don't know her boss's name."

"This is a good start, Ruby. If you think of more, call me, okay? My only mission is to find your daughter."

"Do you want to go through her things?" I ask. "Her notebooks, her journals? They might give us some clues."

"Of course, we would," Huck says. "A forensic team is going to come here in a bit to manage that. I will be here with them, and you are free to help with the ground canvassing, or stay here while people are in your home."

"I suppose I should stay, in case anyone has any questions," I say.

Dodge nods. "And I will head to the school."

I look at Rogers. "After sleeping on it, did you think of any leads for finding Maple?" It feels like a long shot, like if they did they would have led with that, but it is worth asking.

The men shake their heads. "No," they say, "but we aren't going to give up without a fight."

I nod resolutely. "Good," I say, "because neither am I."

CHAPTER 11

Jude

Piper and I spent the last four hours canvassing a specified grid, looking for any clues as to where Maple might be. We found nothing besides a few empty Coke cans and a plastic bag. No signs of our friend.

"Hey," Tara Montgomery calls out to us. I clench my jaw, not wanting to get into a conversation with the class know it all. "Hey, just wanted to check in with you, I know you guys are Mape's besties."

"What did you wanna check in about?" Piper Anne asks. She doesn't say it with any snark, it's as if she is genuinely curious as to what Tara wants to check in on.

Tara gives her a long hug and I watch as Piper Anne just takes it. When she pulls away I see actual tears in Tara's eyes. "I've known Maple since forever too, and I mean we haven't been close since like a fifth grade sleepover, but it's Maple. She can't be missing."

Piper Anne blinks back her own tears. "Except she is missing, Tara. And I remember that sleepover. You told every-one Maple had cooties."

75

Tara groans. "We were kids. Besides Maple was trying to scare me with the Ouija board."

"Whatever," Piper Anne says. "I think it's nice of you to come out here and help look, but Jude and I have to go."

Tara's eyes focus on me. "You are her boyfriend, right?"

"Just her friend," I clarify.

"Where do you think she is?" Tara asks.

"If I knew, do you think I'd be standing here?" I shake my head, irritated. Piper Anne notices.

"Look, we gotta go." She drags me away from Tara and we get in her car. "So you don't like Tara either?" she asks once the doors are closed and we are buckling up.

"I don't like people who try to get in other people's business. It's not that I'm private, but I am protective."

Piper Anne softens. "That's probably why Maple liked you."

"What do you mean?"

She shrugs as she turns on the ignition. "Maple was loyal. Even though she and I were growing apart, she has never made it a thing. It's like she is on my side no matter what."

"Then why do you think she was being so secretive?" I ask, genuinely wanting her take.

"I'm not saying this to hurt you, but I think she was seeing someone else. I think she has always had daddy issues. I mean she has no idea who her dad is. Her mom won't talk about it. So it's like, maybe she was looking for love in all the wrong places?"

I exhale. "You won't hurt me with that. I'm not an idiot. Maple never even wanted to make out. It's like she liked the idea of me, but she didn't actually want *me*."

"I'm sorry," Piper Anne says, her voice soft and hushed. "You deserve more than that."

I meet Piper's eyes and they glisten with tears, filled with understanding. Like she understands me.

"That's nice of you to say," I tell her.

If I could, without crossing lines, I would reach out and take Piper Anne's hand. I would lace my fingers with hers. I wouldn't let go.

As if able to sense a growing intimacy, she lets out a slow groan, frustrated. "So we need answers, because clearly canvassing didn't work so well."

"We will have better luck this afternoon when we go back out," I say, looking for hope in something.

"I hate that I can't log into her Snapchat," she says. "It makes me feel like maybe I'm a shitty friend. I should know her passcode, shouldn't I?"

We got locked out of Snapchat after five failed attempts to enter her username and password.

"And I really thought I had a gold mine with *ChunkyMonkeyForLife*. It's her favorite ice cream and she always makes a 'for life' addition when she texts," I say.

"I thought *MomDodgeMapleThreeAmigos* would work too, I've seen her enter that into her email, which makes me want to get into her computer."

"Maybe Dodge can grab it before the police do," I say.

"Isn't that like, highly illegal?" she asks.

"Yeah, but don't you think you would get more from reading her emails than the cops?"

Piper Anne groans again. "You do realize my own father is a cop?"

"So what do you wanna do?" I ask.

She exhales. "Let's text Dodge." She types into her phone, leaning toward me so I can read what she wrote:

Hey, can we meet up? We need to talk.

He replies right away, *Everything okay?*

She calls him. He picks up right away. "Of course things aren't okay. Your sister is missing. My best friend is gone."

"Right, I know that, of course things aren't okay . . ."

"Thing is . . . I was wondering . . . is there any way you could get Maple's laptop?" Piper Anne swallows. "I know the cops should have it, but I think I can get in it and get answers."

77

"I'm one step ahead of you," Dodge says.

"What do you mean?"

"I got a few things from her room last night. I'm not stupid, I know Maple's secrets are gonna be found online."

"Can you meet Jude and me at Eagle Crest Park?"

"Sure," he says. "I can head there now."

Piper Anne hangs up the phone.

"You want to do this?" I ask her. "I mean your dad might find out eventually."

She locks eyes with me. "You were willing to risk it all with your dad in the hope of helping Maple. I would do anything for her, too."

"You don't think she just wanted to run away, not be found?"

"And just leave her laptop in her bedroom?" Piper Anne shakes her head. "She would never just ditch everything. She's not that kind of girl, the kind of person to just brush everything off, flip the bird to the whole world. She's more serious, more contemplative, more intense. She wouldn't just run away on a whim."

I hear what she is saying, but as we drive toward the park, I try to tease that line of thinking just a bit more. What if, after a lifetime of playing by the rule book, she decided to throw it out? According to her mom and even Piper Anne, over the last few months, she has been erratic. She's suddenly decided her mom is her worst enemy. I have heard her go on and on about how much her mom sucks. How she is a liar. I never pressed — thinking maybe she was on to something, but that was before I walked into her mom's house, where coffee brewed and candles were lit and everything felt cozy and lived in — and not like a monster lived there — like a real-life mom who cared.

She talked about how things felt different with her brother gone at college, and I chalked some of her angst up to Dodge being gone. Maybe the dynamic in the household shifted a lot. I wouldn't know. I didn't know Maple before this year. But maybe it's more than that. Maybe she has secrets. Maybe she is hiding something. And maybe we will find out when we log into this computer.

When we get to Eagle Crest Park, Piper Anne points out Dodge's Subaru in the parking lot.

"Ruby bought it for him, brand new, which is crazy right?" Piper Anne tells me. "Before I didn't realize how much money Ruby made off that book she wrote. But I guess getting your books at every bookstore across America and being a book club hit means you are kind of like a millionaire, which means buying your kid a car isn't the biggest deal in the world."

"They weren't always rich?"

Piper Anne shakes her head. "No, before Ruby published that book she was like on food stamps. Nora and Tom helped out with stuff, they have always been around to help."

I bite my bottom lip, wondering, "What if someone kidnapped Maple to get at Ruby's money?" "Oh, shit. What if? I'm sure my dad's already thought that through but I hadn't."

She parks next to Dodge and we get out of her beat up Honda Civic.

"Hey," I say to Dodge who is leaning against the hood of the car.

He pulls open a backpack that's laying on the hood. He takes out a journal and a laptop.

"No one knows you took those?" I ask, knowing they belong in police custody.

Dodge grins. "I may look like an idiot, but I'm kind of smart. This morning when my mom left to go talk to the cops I took it out of her bedroom, before the cops came to start investigating."

"My dad's been at your house?"

He nods. "Yeah, for most of the day. They went through everything in Maple's room. Were interviewing Mom and me. I wanted to go help canvas this morning but I stayed back with Mom."

"My dad said they were going to talk to me later."

"They wanted me to give a rundown of everything I knew about Maple too," Dodge tells her. "Don't worry, they're not trick questions. They're just looking for her. They're not trying to get anybody in trouble."

"I know," Piper Anne says. "I'll do whatever I can. I just feel kind of like I'm the worst friend ever considering I don't actually know where she might be."

"Well, maybe there's a clue in her journal or in her laptop. But I don't know her password, so I couldn't get into it."

She takes the items from his hand and set the journal back on the hood, and then flips open the laptop, resting it on top of the black journal. The battery is half full and she types in, "Chunkymonkeyforlife." It works.

"What was it?" Dodge asks. I tell him and he laughs. "Maple's such a dork. I would've never guessed that."

"We had a whole dance routine in middle school, C-H-U-N-K-Y. Wanna see the moves?" Piper Anne asks with a smile.

"I can imagine it," he says, cutting her off. "I think you should stick to art."

"Am I that bad of a dancer?"

He laughs. "I remember this so-called routine and I wouldn't call your high kick something to write home about."

Piper Anne punches him playfully in the arm, "Don't be a dick. The dance is cute." Then blinking back tears she amends, "It was cute." She shakes her head. "I can't believe Maple's gone."

"Where do you think she is?" Dodge looks to me.

"No clue," I admit.

"That's the thing," Dodge says. "Huck was at our place all day and I listened to Detective Rodgers, and took in everything I could, and it's kind of a problem."

"What's the problem?"

"Nobody has any idea, anything to go on. No with Lochlan or Brittney either."

That's not entirely true though. I got a voicemail from my dad a few hours ago. The police brought him in for questioning. I don't mention this out loud though. Unless I have

80

more information, I don't want to draw more attention to my father.

"I'm not giving up." Piper Anne tethers her smart phone to the laptop, signaling a Wi-Fi connection. Then she presses her lips together, focusing on the laptop that she's unlocked. Dodge and I watch as she clicks on the inbox, scanning the email.

"Scroll back and back looking for something out of the ordinary," Dodge directs.

Piper Anne rolls her eyes. "I understand the assignment, but thanks."

There's a lot of stuff from the SAT prep course and college admissions and the high school notices. A few things from the club about her new job, and then I see something I don't recognize.

"Who's this?" I ask. "Growler Guy."

She clicks on the email. It's brief. I read it out loud. "I'm glad you found me. Let's meet up."

And it lists a phone number. "What do you think?" I ask.

But Dodge has already pulled out his phone. "I think maybe we have our first lead."

BLAMELESS BUT BROKEN
by Ruby Clarke

CHAPTER 15

Lucy didn't expect to get pregnant two months after meeting Knox. But everything about him was unexpected. This pregnancy was just par for the course. She sat on the closed lid of the toilet in the bathroom of her grandpa's house, staring at the sink. On the counter was a test with two pink lines that she knew were going to change the course of her life, her whole world.

"You done in there?" Knox grunted as he knocked on the bathroom door.

Lucy swallowed, gripping the edge of the countertop, feeling like she was going to heave again and she did. Unable to control herself, she knelt down in front of the toilet bowl, lifting the lid, and emptying her stomach.

Knox opened the door, hearing the retching. "You okay?" he asked, uncharacteristically sweet.

He knelt closer to her, resting a hand on her back, pulling her hair away from her face.

"You've been sick for a few days. Do you think you had the flu or something?"

She sat up reaching for toilet paper to dab her mouth clean.

"It's not the flu," she managed.

Her eyes were wide as she looked at him, this man, who would be the father to her child, their child, this man. She still hardly knew him. Two months in and he was a mystery, except she'd pieced pieces together by then.

He was a dealer. He was operating an illegal business out of her grandfather's house. Her grandfather, who had worked at the lumber yard for nearly fifty years, who got his social security because he put in time working day in and day out, doing his part, paying his taxes.

Knox didn't do things like that and she didn't think he ever would. When she imagined having a husband one day, a family, she imagined someone like her grandpa at her side. Maybe because that is what was familiar, a steady man who always had an encouraging thing to say, who gave her shit, but in a good way, who made her feel confident and capable, who could teach her things like how to change the oil in the car or unclog a pipe in the kitchen sink. She wasn't sure Knox could do any of that.

She didn't think he could even change a tire.

Sure, he fiddled with his motorcycle. But when he was out there, he was mostly shining the chrome or polishing the leather. He wasn't making sure the mechanics of it were working. She wasn't saying Knox was lazy. But he wasn't a hard worker, or at least not the same sort of worker as her grandpa. She still hadn't seen him do an honest day's work. He'd come and go, take phone calls at the landline in the kitchen. Sometimes people would show up on the back porch. He would sell and they would buy and he would come back with cash. But he never gave any of the money to her.

It's like they were living two separate lives still, him sleeping in her bed, her making space for him, accommodating a man she had determined wasn't a good one. Now she looked at him, both of them kneeling on the cold tile floor in the bathroom. This is where she'd grown up, where she shaved her legs for the first time, where she got her first period. This is where she cried in the bathtub until the water ran cold after her grandpa died and everyone was gone and only she was left in this big old house. But then Knox was here and it felt like maybe that was a glimmer of hope, the parting of the clouds, the sun coming through that she'd been waiting for her whole life.

But already she knew he wasn't.

Yet, the test on the counter meant he would be tied to her, linked intrinsically to her for all the days of her life. She swallowed. She looked past him to the test and his eyes followed. He reached for it. Gingerly picking it up between his two fingers, he turned back to her, the test between them.

"It's positive," she said. "The pregnancy test, I'm pregnant."

"Shit," Knox said.

She saw that he was shaking, his hand trembling, fear coursing through him. He was no more ready to be a father than she was to be a mother. Could they do this?

"The timing's bad," he managed to say.

No, *I love you*. No, *You're capable*. No, *We got this*.

"What do you mean the timing's bad?" she asked.

She figured he made enough money that he could support them, buy them groceries and diapers and formula or whatever they would need for this baby, a crib, a car seat. She didn't know anything about kids. But she did know this, that you needed a few things in order to make it work and that she couldn't be working the diner if there was a newborn at home. She'd need a man to help pay her way. Surely what he sold would pay for a life. After all, she was offering their home.

"The timing's bad because, well, I'm in a bit of a pickle."

"A pickle?" she croaked. "What does that even mean?"

She'd never heard him use that word before, pickle. It seemed like a conundrum, like a hiccup, not the kind of trouble that would get in the way of having a baby.

"Maybe more than a pickle," he edited.

"More than a pickle? Then what?" Lucy asked.

He ran a hand over his back, setting the test back down on the counter, turning to her.

"There's some guys after me."

She frowned. "What do you mean *after you*? Could you be more cryptic, Knox?"

He shrugged. "I'm not trying to be."

Lucy stood then, closing the lid of the toilet, flushing it, sitting down. Knox stood up, turning from her. But she saw his face in the reflection of the mirror. They looked at one another like that, her on the toilet looking at him through that bathroom mirror and him looking back, neither of them facing each other. Yet, she saw him.

What she saw she didn't like.

His face was cold and ashen, scared. She wanted a man right now, in this moment. A real man who was brave, who was brilliant, who was wise and kind and big and strong and capable, who could wrap her up in his arms and say, *We've got this. I've got you,* and instead he shook his head at her.

"They're coming for me. I can feel it."

"What do they want?"

"Money," he said.

"How much?" she asked.

"More than I have," he paused. "We could remortgage the house."

Lucy scoffed. "No, we're not doing that. This house is the one thing I have. With it, I'll never have to worry about having a roof over my head. I'm sure as heck not pulling cash out to pay your debts."

"Well, then I'm fucked."

"Okay, well, we'll figure it out. We'll get the money. We'll . . . Wait. Why do they want money?"

"I may have skipped town when I owed them a bunch."

"That's why you came here?" she asked. "To the diner that night? It's why you stayed? You were hiding away from people who were after you?"

He gave her a quick nod. "More or less."

"Well, why didn't you keep your head down, keep your head low? They wouldn't have found you if you had just . . ."

"Look. Selling is what I do. The last few months I still had enough coke from those guys to supply my new customers."

"Is that why they're mad? You stole from their supply?"

Lucy was trying to process. It took her a bit to catch up. She may be a legal adult but she'd never done anything dangerous. She graduated high school, then she went to work at the diner. She paid the few bills she had. She came home. She watched TV. She painted her toenails. She made spaghetti. She looked for love in all the wrong places and now standing in her bathroom was Knox, who wasn't looking for love at all. He was using her.

That night, when they first met at the diner, she could see it all so clearly now. He needed someone to catch him before he fell and she did. With open arms, she let him in. Now she's pregnant with his child. Her child's father is a drug dealer who's on the run for stealing coke and who knows what else?

"What are they going to do when they find you?"

He shrugs. "Like it or not, I'm going to have to find that out."

"How soon?" she asked. "How soon are they coming?"

"Depends," Knox said, running a hand over his stubbly jaw.

He turned around. Now his hands were the ones bracing the counter. He looked at her. "Don't worry. I'll figure it out."

"Really?" she asked. "Do you really think you'll be able to figure it out?"

"You doubt me?"

She swallowed. She didn't want to tell this man who was so much stronger than her that yes, she doubted his ability to solve this problem, that she questioned his skillset altogether, his reasoning, his ability to make rational decisions, his ability to think anything through whatsoever and what the implications of those decisions might be.

"Sorry," she said. "Of course I know you have it. I trust you, Knox."

Her words were lies. They both knew it. But it didn't matter.

"Then we have nothing to worry about," he told her. "I'll figure out a solution to my problem."

"And the baby?" she asked, pressing two hands to her flat belly. "What about the baby?"

He looked at her, not a trace of light or love in his eyes.

"I don't know what to do about that. Can you take care of that problem?"

She swallowed. "Take care of that problem," she repeated, horrified, disappointed, but also feeling like maybe this baby would be the gift she'd been waiting for ever since her grandpa died.

She'd been looking for love and couldn't find it from the guys at school that she hooked up with after her shifts and she certainly wasn't finding it with Knox. But maybe this baby, just maybe, would love her unconditionally and she could love it unconditionally back. It would be a child she could raise in this house, this house that held so many of her memories.

Maybe Knox would leave or get arrested or whatever he was going to do, but it would have nothing to do with her, because she had a baby inside of her and she wasn't going to deal with him anymore. What she was going to do was love this child with all of her heart. She was going to love this child and not let anything get in the way of that, not even this man who was looking at her like she was pathetic.

Because she wasn't pathetic. She never had been.

Maybe she'd been waiting for this very moment all her life.

CHAPTER 12

Maple
24 hours missing . . .

After choking me in the bedroom, he told me to join Lochlan and Brittany in the living room.

I walked, terrified, to where my classmates were. I didn't know them well, mostly because I kept to myself, and I never thought we had much in common. But none of the past matters anymore. Not when we are all at his mercy. Suddenly all that matters is survival.

I want to talk to them, to make a plan, but it is impossible until we are alone.

He forces me into a chair, next to them, and lines us up. Then he puts bags over our head, literal grocery sacks, those paper ones. Using zip ties, he cuffs our hands behind our backs and secures our ankles to the chairs.

He's close by, so even if we wanted to sway back and forth, rocking ourselves, the only result will be us being shoved back upright and maybe a bloody lip. I don't want to risk upsetting him. My throat is already bruised from his grip around it. And he has forced himself on us, refusing to listen to our cries, our pleas for him to stop.

There's tape over our mouths, so we can't speak. We can't say, stop, or you're hurting me, or please, no.

No. No. No.

It's gruesome. All of it. Brittany, Lochlan and I were not friends before this, but I already can sense that they will be a part of my life forever, because they're a part of this chapter.

A chapter too horrific to erase. I hear Lochlan crying. Her sobs don't stop. And it's impossible for me to know exactly what's happening to her in this very moment. But I'm grateful for the reprieve. His hands aren't on me. His fingers aren't pressed between my thighs. He isn't inside of me.

He will be soon enough.

There's a camera propped up in the corner. He's recording all of it. And the way he looked at us before he placed the bags over our heads makes me want to throw up. It's better like this, though. Being blindfolded, not able to see what he's doing, unable to look into his eyes as he does it. I thought I knew him. I thought I could trust him. And this is so much worse than I ever imagined.

When he touches me, I feel a sense of relief. Knowing that means he's not touching Lochlan or Brittany, but his fingers move against me and my whole body tightens. I've never been touched like this before.

I wasn't the kind of girl to have boyfriends in middle school or high school. I never even kissed Jude.

Poor, sweet Jude.

I knew it was wrong to string him along but part of me wanted to be the normal sort of girl who could have a nice golden retriever boyfriend. But deep down I knew that my past meant I would never have normal. I came from a place too twisted for regular.

Before I learned the truth I was happy to stick with Piper, and we did our own thing, probably total dorks, but I love

89

that about us, that we would perfect our goofy little dances on Friday nights and record them for ourselves instead of going out to parties.

We would watch YouTube makeup tutorials and eat Red Vines and drink Diet Dr. Pepper on her bedroom floor instead of going to school dances.

Once I realized where I came from, I started pulling away from her. Not wanting someone as wholesome as her to be associated with someone like me.

And to think my mom was okay lying about all of it. Lying to me and Dodge.

And now it's like I went from being an innocent girl to this. My whole life took a one eighty.

It feels like a nightmare being in that bedroom, and then him coming to get me, making me perform.

Before he pushed us into chairs, he forced us into different positions, into different acts. Throughout all of it, we wore a hood over our heads. And then one by one, he took us out of the room where we're locked in, and he filmed us. With our hands bound to a bedpost, or our feet tied to the chair, anything he can to secure us, to keep us in place. Duct tape over our mouths. Keeping us silent.

And I want to bite him. I want to hurt him. I want to rip off his ear or worse. But I'm also scared because right now as he touches me, I am completely naked, vulnerable on this cold metal chair, him grunting against me. I am at his mercy. He could do anything to me and I couldn't stop it.

I keep my eyes squeezed shut, breathing in and out of my mouth, because that's the only choice I have. Tears streak my cheeks and I'm unable to brush any of them away. My muffled cries for help go ignored. I know Brittany and Lochlan are in equal agony, and I wish I could do something to change the situation we've got ourselves in. None of us thought we'd end up like this.

Alone, at last, back in the bedroom, the duct tape has been ripped off our faces so we can eat the sandwiches he left for us. We don't know when he will be back, but I heard the front door slam shut. We are alone, though locked in this room with barred windows and a metal door.

We can hardly eat, even though we should.

What we should really be doing is starting summer break before our senior year.

Will anyone ever find us?

Even though we are sure we are alone, we whisper, not knowing if there are cameras in this room recording us. Surely there are. Together we try to think of a plan, a way out, an escape.

But we can't come up with anything. There's a large mattress on the floor with some blankets. Last night we huddled together, sobbing. Now, we are wrapped in blankets, trying to warm up. We have nothing on but our bras and underwear.

Lochlan is inconsolable, "I just want to go home. I feel like I'm going to kill myself if I'm here another day. You don't understand, Maple. You've only been here a day. We've been here a week."

"Why do you think he brought me in?" I ask. "After you guys?"

Brittany's eyes are cold. Her hands press against my hand. She holds me tight. "I think he's just a sick pervert. Maybe he's going to get as many girls in here as he can."

"It's awful," I say, "what he's forcing us to do, what he's filming. At least no one will see our face. Except that's what's even worse. You know? He is going to post this stuff online. Some dark corner of the internet. Girls being tortured. Maybe we are even being livestreamed."

"Last week." Brittany whispers, "He kept putting things inside me. I couldn't see."

I don't want to think about it. I squeeze my eyes shut. All three of us terrified.

"Do you think there were girls before us?" I ask.

"There's probably been girls forever," Lochlan says. "He has this whole place set up for this, that camera, the lighting, everything. It's like he's prepared and probably learned his lessons, how best to restrain us."

We fall asleep like that. Lost in our thoughts and our fears. My throat still aches from when he choked me. I can't help but wonder why me, was I so weak in his eyes? Was I always like this? Was he always just waiting and ready?

I wake with a start, to him touching me. He is back, greedy. A monster.

He zip ties me, and Lochlan and Brittany — apparently, we were only allowed a short break. We can't fight him, he threatens us with a razor blade every time we kick or scream. Now, he gropes me until I shake. And then he laughs, squeezing my thighs and my knees. "Good girl," he tells me. "Just like that."

But I don't want to be *just like* anything, especially not for him.

And then he moves to Brittney and I hear her muffled scream of terror. He's doing to her what he just did to me. And it's too much. All of it. I just want to get home. I just want to get back to my mom. I want to say how much I love her and Dodge and Piper and everybody.

In fact, if I get out of here alive for the rest of my life, I swear I will be a good girl. But not the kind that he's talking about. The kind my mom raised me to be.

A girl with a good heart, filled with kindness.

I won't be a bitch to my mom when she asks me how my day was. If I could just get out of here alive then I'll do my best every day of my life. I won't ever keep a secret again.

CHAPTER 13

Jude

Dodge has his mom and Piper Anne has her dad looking out for them. I want to talk to someone who might want to look out for me.

After Dodge called that number at the park, with no answer, I asked Piper Anne to drop me off. I call Mom, even though she has recently decided I wasn't a priority.

My heart pounds. Truth is, the second I press call on her contact in my phone, I get scared that she won't answer.

She picks up on the first ring.

"Hey, Jude, you usually text. Is everything all right?" she asks.

So she hasn't heard.

"It's not all right," I tell her, my voice shaky out of the gate. "Not exactly."

"What do you mean, sweetie?"

"Uh, I don't know," I lie, automatically rejecting the idea of being open with her even though I am the one looking for her attention. "Are you good? We haven't talked in a few weeks."

"Sorry about that, Jude," she says. "I just started a job at a medical transcriptionist office. I've been in training. It's been kind of crazy."

"A good crazy?" I ask, unable to really imagine my mom in this new state, living a whole new life.

"Pretty good," she says. "Though Jonathan's kids are kind of a handful, especially now with summer."

"Right," I say. "How old are they again?"

"Twelve and eleven. Practically twins. Two boys and totally different than you."

"What do you mean?" I ask.

"Honestly?" she laughs. "Between us, they are kind of ass-holes. They are busy with summer camp, but when they get home every night they are all riled up. And a little more macho than I am used to. Jonathan wrestles with them all the time, roughhouses, you know?"

"Right," I say, "and I was more of a comic book and arcade kind of kid."

Mom chuckles. "Remember, you used to go down to Quarters if you got some money? You would play that one game for hours. What was it?"

"The pinball machine," I say. "The one made with the Jumanji theme," I tell her.

She sighs. "And you like those indie movies, the Wes Anderson films. These guys are into stuff like . . ."

"Terminator?" I say.

She groans. "Exactly."

"Well, I'm sure if they're going to summer camp they'll get worn out."

"What about you? What are your plans for the summer?" Mom asks.

"I'm working at the country club in Eagle Crest."

"Oh," she says. "Well, that's a good job."

"Yeah, I'm working at the golf carts and being a caddy. I think I'm going to get good tips."

"Well, that's good," she says, "I'm glad you have a good job going into your senior year of high school and then who knows where you'll end up."

"Well, I plan on going to college," I tell her.

"Your grades good enough for that?"

"I think so and I'll get lots of scholarship money. Dad's pretty broke, you know."

"True," she says. "How is your dad?"

"That's actually the thing I was calling about, Mom."

"What happened?"

"Not like something happened necessarily, but he's down at the police station right now."

"Oh, shit, Jude. What's going on?"

"Well, it's kind of a long story. Are you busy?"

I can hear her driving in the background. She has turn signals that are going and it's like the windows are down. It's noisy.

"I'm fine. I have, like, fifteen minutes before I'm getting home from work."

"Right, well, three girls in town have gone missing from high school."

"Oh. Girls you know?"

"One of them was kind of my girlfriend."

"Holy crap, Jude. Where is she? What's going on?"

"Well, I don't know. The police are looking for her. But it's kind of bad. I'm really scared."

My shoulders start to shake. The tears I've been holding in all of yesterday and all of today are welling up inside of me and now they're pouring out. I'm sitting on this stupid kitchen counter in my dad's stupid apartment where there's no food and nothing to do here except smoke his pot, which I don't even do. Maple's gone and I don't know what to do or when my dad's coming back.

So I tell Mom all of it, about Maple and me, and how she's gone. How we don't know where she went and how Piper and I are scared and her dad's a cop and how Maple's mom's a writer and how Maple hates her mom. But her mom's actually really nice.

"What does any of this have to do with your dad?" she finally asks.

"That's the thing, Mom. Maybe it has nothing to do with him. But . . . ."

"But what?"

"The way he looks at Maple, the way he talks to her when she would come over, it wasn't good."

"How did he talk?" Mom's voice is calm. "What do you mean?"

"He would say things about how pretty she is, how she looked, and she always laughed and brushed it off. I don't know . . ."

"Okay," Mom says slowly, "and you think your dad . . ."

"I don't know. What if he had something to do with it? So I went to the cops and I told them, and then they came down here to get him, to bring him to the station for questioning. He's been gone for about two hours."

"Oh, shit."

"Did I do the wrong thing?"

"Well, what did your heart tell you to do?" Mom asks.

"It told me to go tell a grownup because I was scared. What if Dad did have something to do with it and I didn't say something?"

"I'm not saying you did the wrong thing," Mom assures me. "But if your dad is cleared, well . . ."

"I know," I say. "I'm screwed."

"I didn't say it like that, but . . . ."

"It's what you were thinking," I say to her. "I know. I'm an idiot."

"You're never an idiot for following your heart."

I hear a key in the door.

"Oh, shit," I say. "I think he's back."

"Well, that's a good thing," Mom says with a nervous laugh. "That means he isn't a child molester and running a kidnapping ring in town."

96

"It's true. But, Mom . . ."

"You don't have to stay there. You can always come to Arizona and stay with me. You knew that was an option when I left a year ago. It still stands. If it gets bad there, if he blames you . . . even if it's just for the summer. You have options. You are never stuck. Remember that. It is a lesson that took me too many years to learn."

"All right, thanks Mom," I say. "In the meantime, I might just stay at Piper's or something."

"Will you call me later? Keep me posted?" Moms asks. "I want to make sure you're safe."

"Of course," I say, ending the call as my dad walks into the living room, Detective Rodgers with him. I met Rodgers this morning when Huck drove me into the station. I close my eyes for half a beat, realizing what a long day it has been.

"Hey," I say, shoving my phone in my pocket, looking at my dad, wondering what he knows — if he knows it was me who went to the cops. "What's up?"

I see Huck entering the apartment behind Rodgers and my shoulders fall, relaxed. I feel better knowing there are two officers here. I look past Rodgers to Huck. I want Huck to offer his place as somewhere I could stay. He doesn't. I swallow.

My dad shrugs, walking to the refrigerator and pulling out a can of Bud Light.

"You don't have to stay around anymore, you know," he says over his shoulder to the cops. "If I'm clear to go, you're clear to go too."

My dad's flippant. He's never had much respect for authority and he flops down on the couch, reaching for the remote.

I walk Detective Rodgers and Huck to the door.

"You okay, kid?" Detective Rodgers asks. "The allegations you made today were significant and I want you to know your father has been completely cleared. He had an alibi yesterday morning and last week that checked out. There's nowhere that we think he could be holding the girls hostage. They're not in this apartment."

"Right," I say. "So, I just was an idiot?"

"No, but maybe your dad isn't someone you should stay with."

I swallow. "My mom says I can move down to Arizona."

"Is that where you want to go?" Huck asks.

"Honestly? Maybe," I say.

Huck clears his throat. "Well, if you want to stay at my place right now, you can."

My shoulders fall with relief at his offer. But Officer Rodgers frowns. "I'm not sure that's . . ."

"What? He's a family friend. He goes to school with my daughter. They work together. I don't feel good about him staying here."

I exhale in relief. "Can you just wait? Let me get my stuff."

Officer Rodgers nods. "All right," he says. "But if it's for more than a few days, you're going to have to notify a social worker. You understand that right, Huck?"

He nods. "I get it."

I walk to the kitchen to find my dad.

"What?" he asks, finishing one beer and reaching for another, cracking it open.

"I just wanted you to know I'm going to leave for a few days. I'm going to go stay with my friend."

"Was it you who called the cops? You tell them I'm some pervert, fucking teenage girls?" My dad shakes his head. "I always thought something was wrong with you. You're too soft. Who rats out their own old man for something they didn't even do?"

"I'm sorry," I say. "I was just . . . scared."

Dad laughs. "Yeah, I know. And you think I'm a deadbeat. So you're going to pin anything on me you can."

"It wasn't like that," I say. "I really thought . . ."

"Just leave," he says. "I mean it. Just get the hell out of here."

I don't wait for him to ask me to go again. In my bedroom, I reach for a duffel bag and fill it up with everything I can think of: my laptop, my phone charger, socks, underwear, my uniform and clothes. In the bathroom, I toss in my toiletries, my deodorant, my toothbrush, my toothpaste.

I run a hand through my hair, reaching for a beanie, and pull it on my head. Then I grab my drawing pad and pencils, shoving them in my backpack.

I turn off the light in my bedroom, feeling like when I walk out of this apartment, I'm never coming back. Thank God my dad didn't kidnap those girls and he isn't some creep, but something about him doesn't sit right and I'm not going to spend any more time around people who make me feel like shit.

I got a life to live and I'm not going to spend it with people who are dead set on holding me back.

CHAPTER 14

Ruby

The last thing I need right now is a call from my agent. Chelsea Madison is ruthless, calculating, and so damn good at her job. She's also increasingly persistent at weekly check-ins. I pick up without thinking, instantly regretting it.

"Hey," she says, "so how's the book coming?" Her voice is sing-songy. I'm guessing she's had a glass or two of white wine. I look at the time. On the East Coast it's after dinner. She's probably returning from some fancy-pants restaurant in the city, calling from a taxi cab. I have this inclination because I've been at these fancy-pants dinners with her and I've been with her in the taxi cab when she calls other clients asking for an update.

"Hey, Chels," I say, "it's really a bad time."

"Why? Because you don't want to tell me you have clocked zero additional chapters this week? You know the deadline's coming up. We're going to need something. I need some pages to present to the team."

"No, I get that. It's just, everything is really bad right now," I say. My voice starts cracking.

"The story? Why? Okay, we can go over the plot again."

"No, not the story. My actual life, Chelsea." I swallow. "I don't have chapters done. Yes, the book's shit. Yes, we should probably go over the plot sometime and start from scratch probably actually, because it's all really bad, but—"

"Okay, take a deep breath. Start from the beginning. What's going on, Ruby? Last week you weren't feeling the story. But not like this. What's happened in the last few days?"

"A lot," I tell her. I tell it all. Dodge is upstairs sleeping, which is good because I don't think he got any sleep last night. Earlier he told me he had tossed and turned all night, imagining the worst happening to his sister.

Now, with the house quiet, I give in to the truth, telling Chelsea everything, tears in my eyes as I tell her that Maple is gone.

"Wow, this is all so shocking. It could be a story in and of itself."

"Don't say that," I say, my stomach falling, her words hitting closer to home than she realizes. It's exactly what I've done before, use my life as fodder, and look where it's got me, in a web of secrets, and an agent who thinks I can write a book when I can't.

"But where's Maple?" Chelsea asks. "I mean, actually, where do the cops think she might be?"

"There are no leads," I say. "Well, I guess there was one lead. Maple's boyfriend thought maybe his dad had something to do with it."

"Oh, shit."

"I know, right? Well, the dad got cleared, but poor Jude, how is he supposed to live with the man now that he just accused of being a predator?"

"Holy shit," Chelsea says.

"I know, right? I mean, it's good he spoke up, if he thought that maybe there's some chance that his dad was involved. At least now it's ruled out. But how does that relationship ever get repaired, if you accuse someone of something that they didn't do, something to that extent?"

"Seriously, Ruby, this could be a book."

I hate that Chelsea is thinking in these terms. "Can you not say that again? My daughter is missing. Three girls from town are gone."

"And Maple wasn't friends with them?"

"Not at all."

"Strange, right?"

"Very," I say. "I don't know what links them together or if anything does at all, or maybe they've not even been kidnapped together and it's just a coincidence."

"Regardless," Chelsea exhales, "you need a drink."

"I think I might need something stronger than that."

"All right, well I am sorry for giving you grief for not having gotten any writing done," Chelsea says, "and you're in my thoughts and prayers."

"I hadn't realized you were the praying type," I say.

"Right now," she says, "it kind of feels like you need a miracle."

"A miracle, huh?"

"Yeah. Isn't that what you're always talking about anyways?"

We end the phone call and the word is in my head, 'miracle.' A miracle, how badly I need one. Dodge comes downstairs. "You all right?" he asks.

"You want something to drink?"

He holds up a glass of water. "Just got it. Want some?"

"I need something stronger than that."

He smirks. "Can I too?"

"No, Dodge. I don't do underage drinking. Or drugs in this house, either," I say thinking of my lifelong paranoia with narcotics. So much of my trauma was a direct result of drug abuse. I have always had a zero-tolerance policy in my life because of that.

"Why have you always been so straight-laced, Mom?" he asks. "Kids at school smoke pot."

I shake my head. "You have a bright future ahead of you, Dodge. Don't waste it with drugs. Out of all the things in the world, please, not drugs."

"I didn't even know you cared about drugs that much. You've always been such a chill mom."

"There's some things that are non-negotiable," I say. "I don't want my son in prison."

"Prison over pot? Mom, I don't think you realize weed is legal In Washington state."

I swallow the rest of my thoughts away, not wanting to utter the real horror that is rattling around my mind when drugs are mentioned.

I don't want the adage of like father, like son to be true.

"What?" Doge asks, refilling his glass. "It looks like you just saw a ghost or something."

"Sometimes it feels that way," I admit. "Maybe it's the past coming back to haunt me."

Dodge looks at me. "Mom, why don't you go take a shower?"

"Do I look that bad?" I run a hand over my face, grateful I didn't drink anything stronger after all. I want to be alert, aware, if any news of Maple comes in. "All right. It's not the worst idea. Nora texted earlier and said she was dropping off dinner. "

I walk upstairs to my bedroom, stepping out of my shoes as I walk, pushing down my jeans. I am nearly undressed by the time I get to my en suite bathroom. I close the bathroom door, leaning against it, taking a deep breath. It is hard to stay grounded. The longer Maple is gone, the faster memories resurface.

I step into the shower and turn on the water. My head spins and I realize I haven't eaten all day long. I don't feel sick, just lightheaded. I sit on the floor of the shower, the warm water running over my shoulders through my hair. I close my eyes, wrapping my arms around myself, and remembering my past.

The pregnancy test on the bathroom counter, Knox being in trouble for the drugs, in my belly Dodge was there, already growing. I swallow.

It scares me, that thought, that my past is being replayed. Some karmic lesson gone wrong, and unless I learn, it's going to keep repeating itself.

Oh God, I think, please no. Because Maple's not the only one who has gone missing.

I did too, a long time ago, and the memory of that haunts me still today.

Maybe it's not like father, like son after all. Maybe it's like mother, like daughter.

I close my eyes, letting the hot water wash away the thoughts, knowing that until Maple's back in my arms, I won't have any real answers. I need to know who took her.

And I need to know if it's all my fault.

CHAPTER 15

Jude

Piper Anne looks surprised when I walk in the house with her dad.

"Hey, what's going on?" she asks, her hair is wet and she is wearing pajamas, even though it's only six at night.

"Hey, Piper," Huck says. "I tried to call. You didn't pick up."

She pulls her phone out of her pocket. "Oops. Sorry. It's on silent."

"I meant it," Huck says. "I really want you to have your phone on at all times right now."

"Sorry, Dad. I get it," she says. "Hey, Jude. Where'd my dad find you?"

"At my house actually," I tell her. She's sitting on a stool at the kitchen counter and Huck and I join her, setting down the bags of food we picked up from Burger Shack on our way over here.

"I got us dinner," Huck says.

"Us?" she repeats. "So it's like three of us doing dinner together?"

"Sorry," I say. "It's just . . . I'm not meaning to impose, but . . ." I swallow, glancing behind myself, looking at the duffle bag I dropped by the front door.

"Oh," Piper Anne exclaims. "Are you staying here?"

I nod. "Is that okay? Your dad offered. Things at my place are a little tense." I pull off my beanie and run a hand through my hair. "My dad is cleared. I guess he had an alibi."

"What was it?" she asks.

I look at Huck who answers, "He was at an interview at the car wash yesterday morning. And after that, he went to Labor Ready to pick up a shift. He was unloading a truck of frozen meat at a grocery store all afternoon."

Piper Anne looks at me, and I wonder if she is just now realizing my dad and the life I've had with him is so different than the life she's had with her own father. Her dad is a cop, a steady job. It's not like he's ever out looking for work.

"Does your dad know it was you who tipped off the police?" she asks.

I groan. "He guessed it was me and I didn't argue . . ." I shake my head, hating that there are tears in my eyes. "Damn it," I say. "I'm such an idiot."

"Don't say that," Huck says. "You were doing the best with the information you had. That's all any of us can do in life."

"I'm proud of you," Piper Anne says, piping up as Huck begins unpacking the paper sack of food.

"You are?" I ask.

"Yeah," she says, grabbing one of the fountain drinks we brought back from Burger Shack and shoving a plastic straw into it. "I mean, it was brave of you. What if your dad had done something super creepy and you never spoke up? Just because it's a hard thing to do doesn't mean you don't do it. Maybe if more people acted like that, the world would be a better place."

I smile. "Thanks. I mean it. Thank you for saying that. I felt kind of like a piece of crap and . . ."

Huck claps Jude on the back. "You can keep apologizing and we can keep offering you forgiveness and telling you it's okay as long as you need it on repeat for the rest of the night, I mean it, or we can take this food and go put on some Marvel movie and take our mind off things for a sec."

"You don't have to go to the station?" Piper Anne asks.

"I'm off until morning."

"Is that weird of us though?" she asks as Huck grabs three plates from the cupboard. "Just sitting here watching a movie and laughing while Maple's gone?"

"There are other police officers that are working. Detective Rodgers took a few hours off too. We can only do so much. You know?"

"I guess. But it still feels like we should be doing more." She looks over at me and I feel like I can read her mind. I'm not surprised when she speaks back up. "Hey, Dad."

"Hey, what?" We're carrying our plates of burgers and fries over to the couch where we're going to eat in the living room.

"If Jude can be brave and say things even if it could get people in trouble, I can be brave too," she says, her voice shaky.

"What is it, Piper Anne? What do you need to be brave about?" Huck asks, calmly.

"I have a laptop," she says in little more than a whisper. "Maple's laptop."

I bite my bottom lip, knowing that isn't all she has of Maple's. I am not sure why she wants to hold back that information, but I don't want to say something and get Piper Anne mad at me.

Huck stares back at his daughter. "Wait, you do?"

She nods. "Yeah. Don't be mad."

"I'm not mad. I'm just . . . She leave it here or something?"

As if feeling emboldened, she speaks up, "Dodge gave it to us earlier today. We met up with him at the park, and he got it before you guys went and ransacked Maple's room and the house and everything. He thought maybe I could find something on there that was important."

Huck may be speaking in a calm tone, but he is visibly upset. He tenses his jaw and pulls in a deep breath. "You mean more important than the police having access to this? You do realize there are three missing girls in Eagle Crest. That information on this laptop could help the investigation, could bring your best friend to safety."

"I know," she says, beginning to cry. "That's why I'm telling you now. That's why I'm getting it for you right now." She walks out of the living room, and it is then I realize we made a mistake. Dodge made a mistake too. We're stupid kids.

We should've never let him give us this laptop. We should've given it directly to the police. What if those hours matter more than we know? What if something' bad's happened to Maple this afternoon when we've had this information and kept it to ourselves?

We thought that if we went through the laptop first we might find a clue, something that could be a lead. That we were smarter than the cops.

But this choice could mean a matter of life or death for Maple.

I expect Huck to get even more angry when Piper Anne walks back into the living room with the laptop in her hands, but as she sets it down on the coffee table, he doesn't reach for it. Instead, he reaches for her and he pulls her close and gives her a hug, the kind of hug you need when your world falls apart.

She wraps her arms around him and cries against his chest. "I'm scared. And I know I messed up and I'm sorry, Dad. I'm sorry. You can have the laptop. I'll give you the password and everything. I just . . ."

"I know, baby," he says. "It's scary. You love Maple, and that's why we're going to find her."

"Are you mad at me?"

"You were being very immature."

She steps away and sits on their couch next to me, reaching for my hand. The comfort I feel with her palm pressed to mine cannot be understated. Piper Anne makes me feel like I am not in all of this alone.

"I know," Piper Anne says. "I just got caught up in the moment."

"And Dodge gave it to you because he thought you would have a better chance of finding Maple than me?"

"Maybe. I'm her best friend. I know her the best. But Dad, maybe I don't know her at all. How can I be someone's best friend and not know where they are?"

"That's not what friendship means," he tells her. "Friendship means sticking through things even when we don't understand one another. It means not giving up, having hope."

"I'm sorry, Huck," I say. "You're right, about all of it."

"Is there anything else?" he asks us. "Anything else at all that you're not telling me?"

"No, Dad," she says. "This is everything."

"You're going to have to do dinner alone with Jude. I've got to take this down to the station."

"All right," she says. "I love you, Dad."

"I love you more. And Piper?"

"Yeah?"

"Thanks for being brave even when it's hard."

Huck leaves the house, and I clear my throat, knowing we didn't give her dad everything.

"Should we have given him the journal?" I ask. "You didn't tell him about it."

"That is Maple's most private thing. We could give it to the police, and I know I should, but another part of me wants to go through every single page tonight all on my own because this might be the last thing I have of her."

I nod, not wanting to disagree. "And the laptop's going to have any of her secrets anyways. That email, that creepy one that I don't understand, that's what's going to bring Maple home. Not her journal."

"Maybe it's wrong," Piper Anne says. "But I want that for myself, and I haven't had a chance to read it. I'll read it tonight, and then I'll give it to Dad. I promise."

I nod, not sure if Piper Anne is making the right call. It was courageous to hand over the laptop. But this journal doesn't belong to her. And the longer she holds onto it, the more scared I am going to be.

CHAPTER 16

Ruby

My phone rings as I step out of the shower. Huck. I answer it as I wrap a towel around myself.

"I have something that might have some answers," he says. "Can Officer Rodgers and I come over now?"

"Of course," I say, hopeful. "Come right over."

I end the call and dress quickly, pulling on a pair of jeans and a T-shirt. I towel dry my hair and don't even bother running a comb through it. My heart pounds with anticipation — maybe there is finally a breakthrough. An answer.

Downstairs I look for Dodge, but he isn't in the house. I text him, asking where he went.

Sorry Mom, he texts back. *I needed to get out. I went for a drive. Do you need me?*

No, I reply. *Just be safe. I love you.*

There is a knock on the front door and I open it to find Officer Rodgers and Huck in uniform.

"How did the canvassing go this evening?" I ask as I hold the door open for them to enter.

Huck and Rodgers enter my house, removing their caps. Rodgers runs a hand through his hair. "Look Ruby, I'm not saying this callously, I'm saying it honestly. This picture isn't looking good. Our whole team from the entire Eagle Crest Police Department has been working on it all day and our leads are looking more and more slim. The Brittany and Lochlan cases have ended up in the same place. We've interviewed parents and friends, gone through bedrooms and laptops and iPads. We've talked to teachers and neighbors. It's like the three of them just vanished into thin air. In school one day, gone the next and no one's seen them since."

I blink back tears, wanting to be brave. "Tell me you didn't come here to give me nothing but bad news."

"Earlier this evening Piper gave me Maple's laptop," Huck tells me. "Apparently Dodge took it from her bedroom."

I cover my mouth, shocked that Dodge would be so careless. Something on that computer could have brought us a lead.

Huck shakes his head. "Look, kids are stupid. They're going to do things without thinking it through, and that's what has happened right now. I'm just glad Piper came to her senses."

He shrugs. "I feel like until we find out where these girls are, I can't rest."

"Have you looked at it?" I ask.

"No, not yet," Huck says. "That is what we are going to do right now."

"All right," Rodgers says, setting the laptop on the dining room table. Huck and I sit on either side of him. "Do we know the password?"

"Piper didn't tell me," Huck says. "Let me send her a quick text." He pulls out his phone and fires off a message. A moment later she replies. "Chunky Monkey For Life," he reads out.

My heart tightens. Her password feels like the one a little girl would make. My little girl. Her favorite ice cream opens up the device.

Huck raises an eyebrow. "Okay." He types the password in quickly. "All right, it's unlocked and there's an email pulled

112

up," he says. "It must've been the last thing your daughter looked at."

"What is it?"

"It's from an email address that's just a string of numbers @gmail.com."

"All right, what does the body of the email say?" Rodgers and I lean in, surrounding Huck, reading the email.

I read out loud, "Glad you reached out. I would love to see you."

"And it's not signed," Rogers adds. "Did she reply?"

Huck scrolls down on the page. "It looks like she sent him a Snapchat handle, @maplesyrupsweetie."

"All right, so maybe we've got to get into her Snapchat." I press a hand to my mouth. "I wish we had her phone."

"Well, we can access it other ways, can't we?" I ask. "With her password if we download the app on a different device?"

"Sure, if we can figure out her password," Huck says.

I push my lips out, thinking. "Well, maybe Piper knows it."

"You don't think she's already tried?" he asks.

"You're right," I say. "She probably has, huh?"

"Yeah, I'm sure she's been trying to log in since Maple went missing."

"All right," Rodgers says. "I am going to take this into the station for discovery. Maybe a lab tech can find out her phone password from something they find on this. Or trace the email address."

Rodgers asks Huck if he is heading out too.

Huck shakes his head. "I'm gonna go check on Piper and Jude when I leave here."

"Sounds good," Rodgers says. "And we will all pick back up with the canvassing tomorrow. I heard from the Sargent that a team is going out at dawn."

Rodgers leaves, and I notice Huck hasn't made a move toward the front door. "You want a cup of coffee or tea?" I ask.

He runs a hand over his jaw. "Tea sounds good."

Together we walk into the kitchen and I fill the electric kettle with water, then reach for two mugs and tea bags. Being alone like this with Huck is unfamiliar, but not uncomfortable. When I turn to face him, it's like he is trying to read me. "What?"

He sighs. "There's a lot about you I don't know."

I swallow. "There is a lot about me most people don't know." I don't add that most people do know the facts of my life, they just didn't realize it when they read them.

"It's how I feel about my own past, about my wife, losing her when Piper was so young. There's pieces to my story that I've locked up in a box and thrown away the key."

"Do you ever feel like opening the box up?"

"I have no interest in revisiting the past, not because the memories might not bring me some joy, but because I know they'll also bring me heartache and pain, memories of a life that I thought would've gone different, a life with so much hope and promise."

"Whatever happened in your past brought you Piper."

His eyes lock on mine. "And yours Dodge and Maple."

"Yes, they were worth the bad things that happened to me, a hundred times over," I admit to him.

"Of course. And being a dad to Piper has been a gift, something beautiful, something unexpected. I have been challenged a million times over raising her on my own. It's just never what I envisioned for myself. I pictured something else, a lot more white picket fence, 2.5 kids, a wife, camping trips in the summer and a cruise to Alaska when we retired. A safe, comfortable life, and instead my life ended up being anything but."

I am surprised to find myself relating so much to Huck. "My life ended up being built on shaky ground because it was just me and the kids against the world, the three of us. I had to lay down my own wants over and over again so that I could be the parent they needed."

The kettle is hot and I fill our mugs with the steaming water. We stand there, in the kitchen, a few feet from one another. We could move to sit at the table, but we don't.

"I get that," he says. "I seriously tried to overcompensate for the fact there wasn't a mom around to put her hair in braids or buy her tampons. I've done my best, but maybe there's room in this life for something more than being Piper's father."

I look down in my tea, not trusting myself to meet his gaze. Huck seems to understand so much of me. I wonder what he sees when he looks at me. A woman with her eyes rimmed in red from crying for days, a woman with a woefully tender heart, bruised even. What would it be like for Huck to hold this heart of mine? I suddenly feel exhausted, and have a longing within me to be held.

"Come here," he tells me. He puts his hand out and I reach for it, his fingers clasping around mine. He draws me to him, not for a kiss but for an embrace.

I wrap my arms around Huck. Then, feeling safe, I rest my head against his chest, and I cry and cry and cry.

BLAMELESS BUT BROKEN
by Ruby Clarke

CHAPTER 22

Lucy held the mattress edge, her body writhing in pain as a contraction ripped through her. She tried to piece together the last seven months, the girl she was in the bathroom at Grandad's house, staring at that pregnancy test that was positive, two pink lines, and looking at Knox and having a shred of hope, even though he gave her no reason to hold onto any.

He was in trouble, he'd said, and that was the beginning of what turned out to be a seven-month ride through hell without any indication that it was going to stop once she gave birth. She prayed it would, of course, but she wasn't sure what the endgame with her was for these men.

As the pain ripped through her, as she held on for dear life to the only thing she had, this stupid mattress, she knew she'd be alone with this baby. She knew that if she cried for help, asked someone to come for the delivery, who it would be. And she didn't want any of those men there in that moment. The moment was one that would not be taken from her even though so many other moments had been.

116

Could she do it? she wondered. Give birth to a baby in a room that was dark and cold? Could she manage it? Let her instincts take over and push a child out into this world without any supplies or assistance?

The men who had kept her captive knew, of course, that she was close to giving birth, but no one mentioned a plan. No one came to tell her anything, ever, actually. It was just a rotation of two or three different men. They'd come and take their turns with her. She fought back in the beginning, before she began a new game, a game of silence, of squeezing shut her eyes and disappearing while they took whatever shred of dignity was left.

But at first, she would fight. She would bite and scratch and claw. She would dig her fingernails against their skin until they bled. She would beg, plead, whisper words that might force them to see her as more than a body to be used, but it never worked that way. If she asked for help, they came back at her with a punch, with a slap, pain inflicted that left bruises. Her legs were like a satellite map of the weather, greens and blues and purples. Her body so many shades, her heart growing dark, getting black.

The only thing that kept her holding on at all was this baby inside of her that was growing, with a beating heart. They needed her today and would continue to need her once they were born. And yes, these men were monsters, but would they hurt a child?

She was terrified to find out.

Another contraction ripped through her.

She sobbed as her body shook. She knew she was being loud, too loud for her own good. She couldn't control it though, the way the guttural moans coursed through her, as her body prepared itself to bring a new life into the world.

When Knox had said he was in trouble, she never imagined it would be this bad. But no one could imagine the horror that became Lucy's life.

117

Knox was a bad man. He had stolen cocaine. He was making a profit on the back porch of her grandad's house, and the people he stole from were pissed.

When those men came knocking, Lucy was alone in the house, and she knew it was over. She watched through the living room window as they pulled up to the house. She hid herself in a closet, but her sobs revealed her. Just like they're doing now.

"Take her," he told them, those months ago as they dragged her out of the closet. "We'll take her in exchange for what he owes us."

She wondered if Knox knew. He must have had some idea, at least after, when she was gone. Did anyone come looking? Knox knew she was with child, knew the house was her own, that she had a future, a bright one. She was still saving money for art school. She'd still had that dream that, somewhere deep down inside of her, she could break free from whatever chains Knox had tied around her wrists.

Just because she was having his baby didn't mean she was going to be locked to him forever. But then the men, the drug lords who were after him, came after her. It was easy, of course, to get her in their van, to drive away, for her to disappear. She wondered if the people at the diner came looking. But by then, she figured they wouldn't have. Knox would have told them a story about her skipping town, and they probably would've believed him. Does anybody really come looking after you're gone?

Lucy closed her eyes. She knew the baby was coming fast. She was naked on the mattress, and she pressed her hands between her thighs and she felt between her legs, the baby's head was crowning. She could feel it as its head pushed out of her, through her, into the world. She cried in ecstasy and exhilaration, fear coursing through her as she pushed again and again.

She didn't know what would happen next. Once this baby was born, would these men even come to find out if everything was okay? They were the ones in charge, and while usually she was just something they abused, there were times that their loneliness would look different. Sometimes they would act as if she was a person. They'd come in and they'd just talk to her for hours, confessing their sins and their secrets. Asking what she thought, as if her opinion mattered.

Finding any response at all was near impossible. Lucy would feel her skin crawl and her heart race, not wanting to listen. She wanted out. But she knew if she refused to answer their questions or have a conversation with them, they would punish her. She was tired of being punished. She didn't like the handcuffs. She didn't like the bindings on her feet, and since she'd played nice for so many months, they finally left them off.

If only she could get out of this room. It was a box made of concrete with a metal door. There was a bucket in the corner. Sometimes they brought a gallon of water for her to use to wash herself with a towel, but she hadn't stood underneath the head of a shower in seven months. She was more than a prisoner. She'd become a slave, losing all dignity. Her teeth were gristly. Her hair was oily. Her face was dotted with acne. And now, she was a mother.

A baby was coming into this world and she pushed again and again and again until it emerged into the land of the living. And it cried. It shrieked, which meant it was a breathing, living thing, her living thing. A boy.

She pressed him against her chest, her body bare, her breasts heavy and swollen. Her babe in her arms bloodied and covered in sweat and tears. She knew she would have to deliver the placenta next. The umbilical cord wound from the baby between her legs up into her body, pumping him with more and more life.

She looked into her son's eyes. The room was dark, but her heart was full of light. She may have been trapped in this room for seven months without any hope of escape, but this was something she made. She thought of those paint-by-numbers in her grandma's house, each dot of color representing a bigger picture, and she thought how maybe everything in life works together to make a whole. But she couldn't see the big picture yet. Not with her son, not yet. She couldn't step back and see how the colors might blend to create an image that was pleasing and beautiful. She was looking up close, and all she could see in this image was her child pressed against her beating heart, and she loved him. She loved him. She loved him.

The metal door pushed open. Justice was there.

"Oh shit," he grunted looking at her, light flooding in from the hallway.

"Please," Lucy whispered. "Don't hurt him. It's just a baby."

He looked her over.

"You got to get yourself cleaned up."

His words were ridiculous, as if he knew what was best. She was the one who had just delivered her son all on her own. She had a strength within her she had never felt before.

"I have to deliver the placenta," she said.

He looked at her as if she was speaking a foreign language, and maybe she was, but she didn't care. Instinctively, she pressed her hand to her belly and pushed and bore down, the baby clutched in one arm, her other hand at her center, guiding out an organ that had been giving this baby life for nine months while it was in the womb. She birthed it, and then she laid back on the mattress, her head on her single pillow. She sobbed with exhaustion.

Frank watched. Some other guys she'd been with before came into the room too. She looked over at them wondering what was going to happen next. There's no way they were going to let her out. After all, they'd been torturing her and raping her for months on end. She was their prisoner now, their slave, and everybody in the room knew it. Maybe they never intended for things to go as far with her as they did, but once they brought her here and made her their captive, they crossed lines that would mean either she would die in this room or die trying to escape.

Still, she hoped they would give her just one day with this baby. She longed for so much more. The idea of letting him go was untenable. She would rather die.

"Don't take him," she begged. Even though it was twisted, she knew if they let her keep her son, she would give them whatever they wanted.

"We can't kill a baby," Tommy grunted. Lucy listened to the men debate, grateful that they had a moral compass to draw the line at infanticide, though horrified that they somehow found holding her captive as a sex slave forgivable.

They didn't take her son from her arms. Instead, starting the day the baby was born, they let her shower and they brought in diapers and blankets. She hated them of course, but these items were necessary for their survival. She thanked them, even though the words felt wicked, every syllable of gratitude a lie — she hated them for the monsters they were and yet somehow blessed them for allowing her these gifts.

Of course, later she would see it was Stockholm syndrome. They weren't doing her niceties. They simply didn't want a dead child on their hands. They had already nearly killed the boy's mother. But Lucy couldn't think clearly in that moment.

The day her son was born, the men made sure the baby had what it needed, that she had what she needed. She was given an ice pack to press between her legs, clean underwear, a hot shower, and a comb to run through her hair.

She felt like it was a gift, like they were her miracle. She was brainwashed, of course, to think her captors were heroes, but in that moment, it felt like they were. In that moment, they let her keep her baby.

CHAPTER 17

Ruby

In the morning, I wake with tears in my eyes. I distinctly remember Huck telling me I needed to go to bed, him walking me to my bedroom, him pulling back the sheets and me crawling in. I was still dressed in my leggings and tank top from earlier in the day. I didn't care. I rolled to my side in the fetal position and he pulled the sheet up over me and I looked at him standing there in the light of the moon, filtering through the window thinking, Who is this man?

He is so unlike any man I've ever known. Of course, nearly all the men I'd known were terrible, horrific, the kind of men you don't want anyone to come across, least of all your daughter. I remember thinking that as Huck looked down at me and told me it was time to get some rest. I remember nodding at him, whispering, "Thank you."

He didn't even understand, not even a little, just how much those words meant to me. How much it meant for him to be here at all. He arrived in my time of need, letting me cry against him the way I did. I've never cried against a man like that in all my life, not even once, not even a little.

My grandpa wasn't a crier and we didn't wear our emotions on our sleeves. He was a good grandfather, and did his best to emotionally support me. When I had a bad day at school, he would stop at the Dollar General and get me a tub of ice cream. But mostly, we didn't talk about feelings.

But Huck is different. I've never known a man like him before.

Now I'm in the kitchen. Dodge just made a pot of coffee and is frying up some bacon.

"Oh wow," I say, "This looks good."

"I thought you might need it," Dodge says, with a smile, "protein."

"I stayed up late. It is impossible to sleep. I just toss and turn," I say, grabbing the half-and-half from the refrigerator and putting it on the counter. "Huck was good to stick around and make sure I got to bed."

Dodge turned to me. "You like him?"

"Huck?" I ask.

"Yeah, Huck."

"I don't know, Dodge. He's a good guy. I've just never . . ."

"Never dated anyone? Growing up, you've never had boyfriends . . ."

"I've been busy being a mom," I say.

He rolls his eyes. "Lots of moms go on dates. Get married."

"Well, I'm not most moms. I'm happy," I say. Dodge pours me a mug of coffee, adding the right amount of half-and-half because he knows. He's my son after all. He hands it to me and I catch his eye. He is such a part of me.

"Thank you," I say.

Dodge shrugs as if wanting to say more.

"What?" I ask.

"Nothing. It's just at some point you dated," Dodge says. "You have two kids you know."

"Oh, do I?" I say, rolling my eyes. "I know. I just . . ."

"Look," Dodge says. "I know you get freaked out if I start asking about who our dad is. I'm more than tempted to buy

123

a DNA kit and find out if there is a match out in the world. I deserve the truth."

My whole body bristles. I don't like this line of conversation. There's already too much going on right now. Once we find Maple, I will come clean about all of it, but now, we need to focus on finding her.

"Can we not?" I ask softly.

"It's just . . . I'm almost nineteen years old, Mom. Don't you think at some point knowing who my dad is might be helpful?"

"I've told you over and over again I don't know who your dad is. So I can't exactly give you a name and a number."

He turns back to the coffee, pouring himself a cup. That's how I've always told the story, that I don't know who their fathers are and I couldn't give them names if I wanted to, that I used to get around. I learned my lessons the hard way.

That kind of talk has usually been enough. But everyone's growing up and everything is changing and Maple is still gone and maybe eventually they're going to press for more.

There is a knock on the kitchen door. Nora's face shines through the window. I open the door for her, grateful for an interruption in the conversation.

"Hey," Nora says, walking into the kitchen. "Smells good in here."

"Yeah. Dodge made me breakfast."

"Nice," she says. "You want to eat on the porch?"

I nod. Dodge and I plate up some food.

"Are you hungry?" I ask her.

"Nah, I'll just have some coffee."

She grabs herself a cup, familiar in this kitchen and the two of us head out to the front porch. I pause, giving Dodge a kiss on the cheek.

"Thank you for taking care of me."

And I mean it. How lucky am I to have him here right now, out of all the times he could be home? I need him here with Maple gone. It makes it feel like there's one less thing out of control.

We walk through the house, passing the paint-by-numbers in the hallway. I've put them on a gallery wall. No one knows that they're my grandmother's paintings, things I took from the farmhouse when I finally made my way back there. There was hardly anything left. Most of it had been sold or stolen. But these pictures were in a pile on the floor in the living room and I put them in my car as if they were treasured possessions — because they are.

On the front porch, Nora gives me a tender look. "Tell me how you're really doing."

"Really? How I'm doing?" I press my fingertips to my temples. "Terribly, awful, like I'm not doing enough."

"What *can* you do?" she asks.

I shrug. "It's a good question. The police don't have any leads. Jude's dad was a dead end."

Nora shakes her head. "I've been reading about the other girls, Brittany and Lochlan."

"What about them?" I ask. "I thought about them yesterday. I wondered if I should go talk to their parents at least say hello or . . . I don't know."

"Why didn't you?"

I shrug. "I was too tired at the thought. It seems like a lot of work to go put on a brave face and introduce myself to people who are equally a mess or maybe more so. Their girls have been gone a week."

"It is hard to imagine who could have taken the girls," Nora says softly.

"What do you mean?"

"It's awful to imagine . . . but what if it was a predator . . . someone who . . ." Nora shakes her head.

"Believe me, I have been imagining worst-case scenarios," I tell her.

"One good thing, if that is the case, and I know this is totally against confidentiality agreements and everything, but Tom told me they both got birth control from him last year, IUDs."

"Jesus," I say. "Yeah, you really shouldn't tell me that sort of thing."

She shrugs. "Okay. I just . . . I don't know. Makes me feel better knowing they are protected against pregnancy."

"Maple is on birth control too. She isn't sexually active as far as I know, but I don't want my child getting pregnant. There are dangerous men out there, you know."

And Nora doesn't know the half of it. If I had been on birth control when I had been taken, I wouldn't have gotten pregnant that second time right after Dodge was born. But then again, if I had been, I wouldn't have Maple.

I swallow, looking at her, feeling like maybe I should have been honest with her from the get go, told her my whole truth, my whole story. But I didn't want the kids attached to such a thing. I wanted them removed from that horror show. I wanted a fresh start.

I didn't want to be thought of as the woman who had been kidnapped and raped. I wanted to be known as the single mom who was pulling up her bootstraps, starting over in a new place as far away as possible. When I got in the car all those years ago, and drove away, I wound up on the west coast of Washington.

"I hope the worst hasn't happened," I tell Nora, fighting back tears.

"Hopefully they will all be home soon," Nora says, reaching for my hand and squeezing it. Her eyes are filled with tears too, and I want to open up, all the way, I want to tell her everything, but I am still scared. What if she thinks my secrets are unforgivable? I can't lose her. She is the best friend I have ever had.

"You know how Maple hid the fact she was seeing Jude?" I ask Nora. "Do you think she could have been seeing other men too? If she left campus with someone . . . do you think . . . ?"

"I don't know. I only know what you do. But if she was seeing someone besides Jude I wish we knew. It would help the investigation. I wonder if Piper knows something she is holding back?"

I tell Nora about the computer that Piper brought forward, and the email we read. "She clearly had plans to meet with someone," I say. "I just feel so sick over all of this. And have no idea what is a good lead or a dead end. I feel sick that Jude is already in hot water with his dad for bringing him in as a potential lead. Now Jude's staying at Huck's house because his dad's so pissed at the accusation."

Nora presses a finger to her head. "Damn. It's a mess."

"You're telling me," I say. "I just want my little girl home."

Nora looks at me, her eyes rimmed in red and I know she's feeling the weight of all of this too.

"If you want to get Maple back then don't leave any stone unturned. If Piper has an idea, some clue about where she might be, maybe she'll tell you. Maybe she couldn't tell her dad. Maybe she was too scared or embarrassed. You have to try, Ruby. Do it for Maple. You know that miracle you're always talking about? Why don't you find it yourself?"

CHAPTER 18

Ruby

Detective Rodgers pulls up in his cruiser as Nora is getting up to leave. I reach for her hand. "Maybe there is news." I feel a hopefulness rise up within me.

But as I take in Officer Rodgers face as he gets out of the car, it's clearly grim.

"Just give it to me straight," I say to him as he steps up to the porch.

"We have no news," he tells me. "I wanted to come check on you though, see if you thought of anything else that might help us."

I press my fingers to the bridge of my nose. "That isn't good enough. Surely you found something on the computer?"

"Not yet, but we are still looking into that."

"Who was she meeting? Who was that person she was emailing?"

He looks at Nora then me. "I wish I had better news. There is a search party out right now at Eagle Crest Park if you want to join them. It might feel good to do something tangible."

"That isn't enough," I say, feeling trapped all over again, like there is no way out of this hell.

Walking away from Rodgers, I am exhausted, the ache in my heart from not having Maple here feels unbearable.

Rodgers walks back to his vehicle, and Nora takes her leave too, promising to call and check in later. As I close the door, I think about what he came here to say.

We have no leads.

I don't know what kind of detective he is. But I feel like he's doing a really mediocre job. I walk down the hall into the living room. Dodge is sitting on the couch, playing a video game. "Who was that?"

"Officer Rodgers."

"Any news?" Dodge asks, pausing his game and setting the remote down, giving me his attention with anxious eyes.

"None," I say. "Maybe Huck will know something." I shake my head. "It almost feels like they're giving up, like they don't have any hope, so they're just quitting."

"There was nothing on the computer that could give him a lead?"

"Well, there was that email. But I guess it's come to nothing so far, which makes sense. People send anonymous things on the internet all the time."

"I think Piper and Jude were trying to get into her Snapchat," Dodge tells me.

"Did Piper tell you that?"

"Yeah, she texted earlier, sounds like her and Jude are losing hope. Maybe we should all go out and walk the streets looking for her. I feel like I am useless just sitting here."

"Me too," I say, sitting next to my son and giving him a hug. "I feel like there's pieces I don't know and I wish I did, like whatever Maple's been really dealing with these last few months when she's been so absent from me." I shake my head. "Something changed and I want to know why."

"Teenagers can get moody," Dodge says. "I mean, I'm nineteen and I'm still all over the place."

129

"But this is different. It's like two months ago, Maple disappeared, not physically, but emotionally. She just completely withdrew. There has to be something that was the catalyst for that."

"When I see Piper I am going to talk with her, see if there is something she knows that she hasn't revealed yet."

Dodge suggests we get on our shoes and head over to Eagle Crest Park where Detective Rodgers said he has a search party unit working today. Together we get in my car and drive the short distance. When I park, I see I have a missed call from Nora. She didn't leave a message or text, so I slide my phone in my back pocket and close the driver's side door. As we cross the parking lot, Huck waves us over from a portable police unit. We walk toward him and he gives me a warm smile. "Holding up okay this morning?"

I exhale. "Barely."

He nods. "I can only imagine. Your timing is good. Lochlan's parents are here," he says, pointing to a couple holding paper coffee cups and speaking with Officer Rodgers. "Can I introduce you?"

Dodge and I nod and head over to them. Huck introduces them as Tiffany and Jonathon, and she reaches out to give me a hug. I am not an overly touchy person, but I understand that in this moment human connection is something to cling to. We are in the midst of horrific pain.

"I'm so sorry about your daughter," I whisper. "I can't believe this is happening."

"We haven't given up hope," Jonathon says. "God will bring home our girls. We will have them in our arms soon."

I wipe the tears from my eyes, surprised at the comfort found in his faith. "I hope you are right. I am looking for a miracle."

Tiffany nods. "We all are. We were with Brittany's parents last night, and all of us seem to trust our girls will be back. Brittany and Lochlan have been best friends for years, and are outgoing, opinionated girls. Whoever took them, they won't give up without a fight."

I think of Maple. Would I call her outgoing? A better suited word to describe her might be tender. There has always been a longing in her, a depth. Like she was searching for something.

Someone.

I swallow, wishing I had been more open with her and Dodge. Wishing I had found a way to tell them the dark details of their origin story.

Huck tells all of us that we can go out to designated areas to search. Dodge and I get assigned a section of the park and head off. We silently walk for over an hour, in tandem, both of us lost in our thoughts. The park is massive, sprawling trails that are covered with conifer trees and mossy logs. Ferns that are so bright they are practically neon offer bursts of color to a very heavy day. There is nothing that indicates Maple or anyone else have walked this route anytime recently. Eventually we finish the assigned section, my heart less hopeful than when I began.

When we make it back to my car I ask Dodge how he is doing.

"I'm scared, Mom."

"I know," I say softly. "So am I."

"You know how Lochlan's parents said they had hope?" he asks.

I nod. "Yeah, why?"

He shrugs as we get in the car. "I don't think I have hope like that. If some monster really kidnapped my sister . . . it makes me think there is no good in the world at all."

I shake my head. "No, don't think that is true. One bad person, or even a lot of bad people, don't account for everyone."

The way he looks at me tells me he doesn't believe a word I say. And as I start the ignition, no closer to finding my daughter, I wonder if he is right.

CHAPTER 19

Ruby

There is a knock on the front door just as I am taking off my shoes back at the house. Dodge is sitting on the couch with his phone.

Frowning, I open the door, finding Nora there.

"Hey," I say. "I wasn't expecting you."

"Is it a bad time?"

"Of course not," I say. "There's never a bad time with your best friend."

She's holding a manila file. I saw her only a few hours ago, but she looks different. Jittery somehow.

"Can we talk alone?" she asks, seeing Dodge.

"Uh, sure" I say and we head to the kitchen. "Of course." Once out of earshot of Dodge, I turn to her. "Do you know something, something about Maple?"

She swallows. "I don't know if it's about Maple exactly. Uh, more like it's about you."

We're standing on either side of the kitchen island. It's a butcher block counter, where I've been cooking, trying out all sorts of new recipes lately when I haven't been able to get anywhere with my book. I'll come into this kitchen and pull out vegetables and make a pot of soup, chopping them all up, or bake a pie, bake bread. My hands rest on the counter now, feeling antsy, wondering if I will ever type again. The story doesn't want to be written and Nora's looking at me like whatever she's going to say next is just going to push me further away from finding any creativity. How could I be creative now when my daughter is missing, when a detective has no hope? I'm bracing myself for the worst, feeling a growing tension between Nora and I.

"Just get out with it," I blurt.

"Okay. Okay. I just . . ." She pauses, tucks a strand of hair behind her ear. "I don't want to upset you."

"I'm already upset," I tell her softly. "Maple is gone and it feels like my whole world imploded."

"The thing is," she says, "I did some digging."

"Into Maple?"

Nora shakes her head. "Into you."

The room seems to pause. My mouth is set in a firm line. I knew this day would come. In fact, I'm surprised it hasn't come before. Especially after the book was written. I assumed something would click for someone somewhere, that my story would be recognized as something not so outlandish, that someone might see me in Lucy, see Cory in Knox, remember my grandad. That they would connect dots, find threads and piece them together.

But no one did, no one but Nora, now. I see it in her eyes when she looks at me.

"Well, after I left your house this morning, I decided to take a long walk. I parked my car downtown Eagle Crest and began on the far side of town, thinking I'd wind around the inlet and then make my way to the main street. I needed to stretch my legs and let myself think."

"About Maple?"

She shakes her head. "Not really. Mostly I was thinking about you. I spoke with Tom last night, about how after all these years there are so many pieces missing from what I know about you. I was wondering why."

I press my lips together. "You were talking about the same thing in my kitchen a few nights ago."

She exhales. "As I walked along the main street, I just kept wondering what's happened to Maple and Lochlan and Brittany. Three girls gone. I don't want to keep pressing you about your past, but I'm your best friend. If I can't ask that, who can?"

"I know I've withheld a lot over the years—"

She cuts me off. "It's more than withholding. It feels like secrets. It's lies. And maybe I'm projecting and I'm wrong and we're all processing things differently, but it makes me question everything since the beginning of our relationship, why you've been so private."

"I never meant to hurt you," I say truthfully.

"I hope not. But Ruby, as I walked past the waterfront to the main street, I paused at that bookstore on the corner." She steps back, leaning on the kitchen counter, looking intently at me. "I saw your book in the window, *Blameless But Broken*. I stared through the window looking at the cover. I've read the book before, of course. Everyone has. But I found myself walking into the bookstore and picking up the copy that was on the front table, next to the stack of books, *autographed by a local author*. I took the copy and opened a page at random. It was Chapter 22, the chapter where Lucy, the main character, gives birth to her son."

"I know the chapter, Nora, I wrote it." My whole body is tense, feeling like I am being caught, but she isn't speaking unkindly to me. Nora is being cautious with her words, thoughtful. As if she is opening Pandora's box and is curious about what might spill out.

"It's a terrible chapter seeing a woman give birth in such horrific circumstances," she continues. "But, ultimately, it ends with her feeling a sense of hope. Even though she's forfeited her whole life after meeting this man, Knox, she has a child in her arms."

"What are you trying to say Nora, just say it."

She nods, reaching for a water glass in the cupboard and filling it from the faucet in the sink. She takes an agonizingly long drink before continuing. "I stood in the bookstore, considering the story, considering you, the author, wondering where you got this source material. It's a question that's been asked of you many times. I've heard you in interviews and I've read the articles, and I've even talked to you about it. And you always say, 'The mind is a mysterious thing.' You told me you imagined a worst-case scenario and wrote about it. The worst-case scenario you could think of is bringing a child into the world, being locked in a room without any security, any safety, any food, any toilet. All of it is just one bad thing after another. It's like torture porn that nobody can seem to get enough of." She shrugs, setting the water glass down. "I couldn't. I read that book so quickly when it came out, it was like I was watching a horror movie. And that's how it was categorized, a horror thriller. I didn't even know that was a genre before I read this, which is probably part of the reason it had such a big appeal. It was cutting edge. It broke convention. It was worst-case *everything*." She smiles. "You think it's a love story the way Knox walked into Lucy's life and swept her off her feet. But soon it becomes a nightmare that becomes worse and worse with each chapter. By twenty-two, when the main character Lucy gives birth, you have already read in detail about her being raped, about her being humiliated, about her being harmed, the way her captors would physically and emotionally abuse her."

I stand so still, waiting for her words to end, but she keeps going. I know then she isn't going to stop, won't let me off the hook. And she shouldn't. I have held back for far too long.

"The whole time she's carrying this child and as a reader you're terrified," she says. "You're scared, wondering if the baby's going to make it and then it does, and it takes its first breath and it cries and its cry brings in the captors, Justice and the other guy, what's his name? Well, they give her the gift of

135

a shower as if somehow washing away the blood after birth is going to make everything better. But even that scene is horrific to read because she steps into the shower and hands her baby over to Justice, the man who has forced himself onto her how many times already, and now he's holding the most precious thing in the world and she's got to bathe. She's got to wash the sweat and the blood off of her body."

"I know the story, Nora. You don't have to retell it word for word."

She holds up a hand, stopping me. "I remember reading about the way she gripped the edge of the shower curtain, watching as the water ran over her, the first hot shower she'd had in seven months, her greasy hair and her dirty fingernails. As she watched Justice, her abuser, hold her newborn baby in his arms, and you read about the spot of tenderness she felt for him. The way he looked with this child, it was gruesome and it was raw and it felt real. And as I flipped those pages, standing in the bookstore, I knew why those emotions felt so real. It wasn't a novel at all. This was your life. It must be."

Tears fill my eyes and I press a hand to my mouth, thinking of other scenes, of the way Lucy was shoved in the van four months pregnant and kidnapped by those drug dealers. I squeeze my eyes shut trying not to remember.

"I turned the book around to read the back jacket," Nora tells me, stepping closer, reaching for my hand. "There was your face. Your author biography is brief. *Ruby Clarke lives with her two children in the beautiful Pacific Northwest.* That's it. Nothing about where you went to college or where you grew up or what your inspiration was or what your credentials are."

I can't speak. I feel numb and nauseous. Nora's hand wraps around mine. She figured it out but she isn't walking out the door. She is here.

"I don't know why it took me so long to see. On the first page it was clear," she says, slowly, opening the copy she has in her hands, reading out loud. "The maple tree-lined streets and the Dodge pickup your grandpa drove. I should have seen the connection. You named your children after two of your favorite things from your childhood."

I swallow. "What are you trying to prove? That I kept secrets. You're right Nora, I have. I have already suffered enough, do you want me to suffer more?"

"I don't want you to suffer at all. But I want to find Maple. And I couldn't help but wonder, what happened to Knox? Where is the man that got you pregnant? Where did he go? I know what happens to him at the end of the story. In the novel, I know what Lucy did once she got free. But if the timeline of the book is correct and Lucy escaped her captivity when pregnant with her second child, that means whatever happened to Knox happened seventeen years ago. Because that's how old Maple is, which means Knox could be free, which means Knox could be closer than we think."

"What are you saying?"

"I started looking online. I started in Tennessee, where your book takes place. I couldn't find anything there, so I started casting a wider net. I landed in Pennsylvania. And seventeen years ago, there the story was big enough for plenty of articles to be written about it. There was a trial, and a guy went to prison, a man, Cory, for drug charges and then for assisting kidnappers in holding a woman named Tilly hostage."

I swallow. "What about Tilly?" My eyes find Nora's.

Her gaze is set firm on me. "Tilly was pregnant when she was first kidnapped. She gave birth and then got pregnant again. She escaped."

I swallow. "So you're a detective now?"

She shrugs. "Why didn't you just tell me the truth? You've been through hell, Ruby or Tilly or Lucy. I don't even know what your name is. Do I even know who you are?"

"I'm Ruby," I tell her. "Tilly died a long time ago."

Nora looks at me with eyes full of tears.

"Don't," I say, knowing she is reaching out, wanting to pull me in close, and my first instinct is to pull back. "I don't need your sympathy. All that happened in a different life."

"But it is your life. Why did you write it like it was fiction?" Nora asks.

"Why does it matter?" I say. "It's a story I needed to tell and I didn't want to tell it as if it was my own. That would've made it too sensational, too unnecessary."

"The thing is," Nora continues, "Cory got sent to prison."

"Yes," I tell her. "I know. I sent him there. My story, my helping the police is what got him behind bars."

"And how long was he sentenced for?"

"Twenty years."

"Do you know what prison he's at?" Nora asks.

"Yes, but what does it matter? This is all . . ."

"I know. It's all in your book, in a book that people read and think is make-believe. But it's real. All those horrible things that happened to Lucy in that novel happened to you." Tears stream down Nora's cheeks and she shakes her head. "You're my best friend. You have been for a decade and I didn't know any of that and now . . ." She swallows. "If you had just come clean, if you had just told me the truth, I might've been able to look into this sooner."

"Look into what?"

She hands me the folder. I open it and sitting on top are the discharge papers. I look up at her.

"No," I say. "This can't be true."

"It is. Your ex, Cory, the one you sent to prison, the one you call Knox in your novel, he's free."

"What do you mean free?" I repeat.

She swallows. "I mean, he was released from prison six months ago, which means . . ."

I cover my mouth in horror. Just then Dodge walks into the kitchen.

"What's up?" he asks. "I was just hungry and . . ."

Nora shakes her head. "It's not a good time."

"Okay, but . . ."

Nora watches as Dodge walks closer to me. "Mom, what's going on? You can tell me. You know I have your back always."

I swallow. "Thing is, Dodge. I may not have been completely honest."

"Honest about what?"

"Everything. Your sister, Maple, she might be with your birth father."

"Wait, what?" He runs a hand over his jaw. "My dad, the man you say you don't even know, has been around all this time? And you never told me, Mom, you've lied to me my whole life. You've withheld all of this?"

"I had to protect you," I say.

He looks at me with anger in his eyes. "Protect me by lying to me? That's not how it works."

"But what if it *is* how it works?" I push back.

He looks at me with shock. "You think Maple's with this guy?"

"We don't know," Nora tells him, then looks at me. "But I think we need to find out."

"Maybe it's who she was emailing," I say, shaking my head. "If she was, if they went off together, if my little girl's with him . . ."

I suppress a sob, squeezing my eyes shut and looking up to the heavens.

"This can't be happening," I whisper. "How did I miss the warning signs?"

139

CHAPTER 20

Ruby

Dodge stands in the doorway of the kitchen. "Why didn't you just tell me?" he asks. "Why keep who our father is a secret?"

I look from my son to my best friend and back to my son. And I realize all these years of keeping a secret got me exactly nowhere. Here he is looking at me as if he doesn't know me at all. And the truth is maybe he doesn't because the things I've kept to myself, the things that I wanted buried, were because I wanted to protect him.

After all, isn't that a mother's job? Isn't that my one task?

And maybe I failed my children because Maple is gone, taken out of thin air just like I was. And maybe history is just repeating itself. And this is a horrible karmic lesson for keeping my mouth shut for so long.

But even when I tried to tell my story, when I started typing it out detail by excruciating detail, what came out of me was a third-person account, a fictionalized version of my reality. Maybe I did it like that for self-preservation, because claiming my story as my own felt too brutal, too sickening, too harsh, because then my children would know the truth about where they come from, who Dodge's father is and the fact that I don't know who Maple's father is.

And what kind of mother am I anyways for keeping secrets like this yet telling the whole world in an encrypted version of my truth?

They deserve more, don't they?

I know they must because when I look at Dodge now, it's like he doesn't even recognize me. It's the same way that Maple has been looking at me for the last few months, which makes me think Nora is onto even more than I realized.

Dodge steps closer. "Mom, you've really known who my dad was this whole time?"

I swallow. "Yes." And I press a hand to my mouth wondering what Maple thinks, desperate to know where Maple is. "I couldn't tell you," I tell him.

Nora, though, won't have it. "You were able to tell the whole world."

"What does that mean?" Dodge asks.

This is a defining moment when either I step into the light or shrink and hide. So much of my story has already been decided for me without my consent but this part, I can choose.

"The book I wrote, *Blameless But Broken*," I say. "It was a real-life account." I choke out the words, tears stinging my eyes. And Nora, like the best friend she always has been, reaches out and takes my hand across that island and she squeezes it and she doesn't let go.

Dodge looks at me with bewilderment. "Mom, you're joking. That book, that book is horrible."

"It was a bestseller for a reason," Nora says, "because it's unbelievably horrible."

"Except," I say, "it is believable if you lived it. Like I did."

"All of it?" Dodge asks, pressing me. I wonder what part he is imagining right now. Which awful scene first came to mind. My chest hurts from the agony of this confession. I never wanted to hurt anyone, especially not my son.

141

"Everything in there was true. I changed some things, names, dates, towns, states."

"It's your whole past?" Dodge asks. "The whole mess of it is your actual story, Mom?"

"Yes," I say.

"My dad," Dodge's voice cracks. "He was . . ."

I nod. "In the book he was named Knox. His real name is Cory."

"Why would I believe you now? You spent my whole life telling me that you don't know who my dad was and you did this whole time. You kept this from me."

"What did you want me to say? That your father was a monster . . ." I swallow, tears pooling my eyes because the other part is even harder. "And it wasn't just about protecting you, it was mostly about protecting Maple because . . ."

"Because you don't want Maple to know her dad is a rapist."

"Exactly," I say. "And how does a mom explain that? It's better to leave those pieces unsaid."

"Is it, though?" Dodge asks. "We're entitled to know the truth of our lives, Mom. Hiding it, telling lies about it, doesn't protect us. And then, God, you told the whole world."

"I had to tell the story," I sob. "It was eating me up inside. I had kept it buried for so long. I needed to let it free. I needed to let it go."

"You could have written a journal," Dodge says, scoffing and looking at me with disgust.

"Don't," I say. "Don't pull away from me. I've already lost so much."

"Did you? Because you made millions off this book, Mom. You're set for life."

"Off what? Of the horrific things that happened to me," I say. "The first chance I got, I left so I could protect you and your sister. It's all I wanted. I've been doing this on my own ever since because I love you." I pull my hand from Nora and I press my hands to my face, sobbing against my palms both horrified and terrified.

"If Maple's with him, I don't think you understand how bad it is," I say. "He's not just a bad man. He's a monster. They all were. They all are."

"I don't know who else is out of prison. I think it's just Knox, err, Cory," Nora says. "He wasn't actually holding you hostage. It was the other men. And one died."

"I know," I say. "And he got a much longer sentence. I think thirty years. But Cory . . ."

"What, he got released on good behavior or something?" Dodge asks.

"Yes, actually," Nora says. "Exactly that."

"So my dad's not in prison, but how do we know he's here in Eagle Crest?"

"Well, I was able to look him up," Nora says. "He's not hiding the fact he's around. He has a Facebook profile and there was a picture of him at a coffee shop in Travistown. That's only like twenty miles away."

"When was that photo taken?" I ask.

"Two weeks ago. There's other ones from the area too. I think he relocated here. Maybe he found out where you lived and . . ."

"Maybe," I say, "but maybe he has nothing to do with this at all."

"Mom, don't be crazy. Of course he has something to do with this. How could he not? If he's local and he's out of prison and he's from our past, and Maple's now gone. It's too many coincidences."

"Sure," I say, "but why wouldn't she tell me?"

"Well, why didn't *you* tell me?" Dodge pushes back.

"There's one more thing," Nora says. "Piper Anne says she left school with someone. That she was being secretive about it."

"You think it was my dad?" Dodge asks.

Nora sighs. "I'm just telling you what I know. I'm not going to make any guesses. We need the police for that."

"Mom," Dodge says. "I don't know what to think right now, but I do know this, we need to tell Huck and Detective

Rodgers what's going on. We've got to get Maple back because if everything you wrote in those books is true and that man is free . . ." He swallows. "You know he's coming after her. He's going to be looking for payback."

BLAMELESS BUT BROKEN
by Ruby Clarke

CHAPTER 26

None of it was how Lucy imagined motherhood would go. She'd been in this room for one entire year. She carried a baby to full term, gave birth to it, and now two months later, she was still here, holding that same baby in her arms. He was the only thing that mattered. Ten pink fingers and ten pink toes and a mop of black hair. She'd kiss his tiny head and think how he was just like his father, with all that hair. She prayed that was their only similarity.

Knox's disposition was not something she wanted replicated in this little boy who was so near perfect it made her heart ache. They'd gotten more lenient, the captors. They'd let her bathe and let the baby bathe too, every other day. That was a massive change. But soon she realized why they wanted her to stay cleaner.

They had use for her still. They brought in a basket for the baby. It was a woven thing, and she knew he wouldn't last in it long, not as soon as he started moving, but he hadn't started that yet. He was still so small.

Mostly, he was in her arms. She tried to remember songs from her childhood, but everything from before this room felt like a bit of a blur, a haze. All she could remember was pacing the space, wishing she could get out, wishing she was free, but knowing now, she was even more vulnerable than before. Before she'd been pregnant, but now she had this baby. Any hopes of escaping seemed impossible, seemed like a fantasy. And right now, she was living nothing but a nightmare.

She'd hold the baby in her arms. She named him Lucas after her. Both Lucy and Lucas meant light, and that's what she was clinging to. Something she hadn't seen since she'd been moved into the space and God, she wanted it. She wanted that miracle. The miracle of sunlight on her face, on her baby's skin.

She wondered if her skin could get any more pale. Sometimes when she was in the bathroom and she'd look in the mirror, she felt translucent. The freckles on her skin looked like constellations, they were the only bright spots. Everything else felt dark.

Those last few months before she gave birth, they hadn't been as greedy with her body, but now, now it's like they set a new intention for her. Her breasts were full. Her milk was in. She knew she had extra curves to her body and the way they looked at her when they would bring diapers or take out the garbage, there was a thirst in their eyes, a hunger, and she knew why.

These men weren't exactly ugly. They were men in their mid to late thirties, and certainly they could find someone to date, but then again, maybe not, because at their heart, these men were monsters. Any woman would see through that pretty fast, so maybe she was all they could pull, all that they could have, and so they would take her for what they could get.

She hardly had anything to wear. Neither did Lucas. At some point, they had brought in a bag of used clothing for her and baby clothing for him, from what seemed to be a thrift store. The tags were still on, priced at 49 cents and 99 cents. Onesies and pants, basic things. She wanted socks for his feet. She thought that's what a mother would do, put socks on her baby's toes to keep him warm. She didn't have socks for him though, so she made do. She would pull him against her chest, and roll to her side and he would nurse until he fell asleep. She would sing him lullabies from a childhood she never even had, a life that seemed so far away.

But then, of course, the men were patient no longer. It had been two months. Her body must have healed. They knew what they wanted. They walked in the room and told her to put the baby in the basket. She shook her head, scared. She wasn't ready. But she knew it was coming.

If they were going to have her, this was it. This was why earlier in the day they had told her to bathe. They'd even put a razor in the shower, and she used it. She had held that razor in her hand and considered not using it, she wished she could resist it, but she wanted to be clean. It had been so long, and the hair on her legs was long and under her armpits too, and she just wanted to feel scrubbed. She wanted to feel something besides used.

But the razor and shower weren't gifts. It wasn't so she could take care of herself. It was so she would be more ready to receive them. Three men entered the room and she tried to close her eyes, but she was scared of losing sight of Lucas, who was sleeping in the basket in the corner.

The men didn't care that a baby was there. Lucas was oblivious, and she prayed he always would be.

What happened to Lucy next was a story that was etched in her memory in a way that felt like a scar. Maybe it was deeper than that. It cut so deep she should have bled out. She wished in that moment she could die, but then she'd look over and she'd seen Lucas and she would stop wishing for that, and instead, she just wished it would be over, but it wasn't.

It was so long. It was so much. It was three men against her, taking her.

Her body was tender. Her breasts were sore. She wanted her baby in the fresh air and the night sky and hope in her heart and a promise for a new day, a new life. She wanted anything else. This couldn't be her forever. It couldn't. It wouldn't.

Yet still, they took parts of her she hadn't ever been offered to anyone. Parts that really never had been given because now, they were just simply taken. They were rough and they were harsh, and they moved against her with a sense of urgency and power. They held a sense of control that she couldn't compete with.

In all her life, she'd never even considered simply taking what she wanted without asking permission. But these men had no problem doing just that.

It was more than an undoing. It was such an unraveling that after, she felt as if she had vanished. She cried that night, holding Lucas to her chest, wanting that to be the end of it. But no, those men were hungry and they knew what they were craving, and it was her.

And she wondered if this could even be called living, what was happening to her. Yet somehow she was, because after, they would allow her to take a shower and she would scrub her body clean, and then she would move toward her son, holding him, crying against him, praying for a miracle.

That's all she wanted, was one tiny miracle.

She wanted to be free.

Of course, by then, she felt it.

The moving in her belly, the new sign of life, the nausea returning. She was pregnant once again. This time, it wasn't Knox's baby.

This time, she had no idea who the father was. It could be any number of monsters.

CHAPTER 21

Jude

I'm not saying I think the police are stupid. I mean, Piper Anne's dad is a cop, and I have faith in him . . . I think. But they aren't coming up with leads. Which means Piper Anne and I have got to do something.

"There's no way whatever secrets Maple has buried are all stored on her laptop." We are in Piper Anne's bedroom in the middle of the afternoon. The hours tick by so slow. It is agonizing not knowing what to do.

"Why not?" I ask.

"It's just not how she would have done things. She only used her computer for schoolwork, and she didn't even really like school. It's not something she really used, unless she was writing a paper for English. She was always on her phone."

"We need to figure out what her Snapchat password was. Then we'll know who she was talking to. She used Snapchat more than texting even."

"Well, we only have one more chance before we get locked out, again." I say as Piper Anne starts flipping through Maple's journal, looking for a clue.

149

"Um, I know it was wrong to not hand over this journal to my dad," Piper Anne says as she runs her hand over a page, "but my instincts were right."

"What do you mean?"

"Look?" She hands it to me, and when I scan the pages of her journal, the answer is literally right in front of me. Written on a random page, in between doodles and sketches, notes about what school assignments she needed to complete so she didn't fail eleventh grade was a simple passcode and one that I ask Piper Anne about. "What does Iamthemiracle mean?"

"*I am the miracle* is a phrase her mom would say. She would tell us girls to say it to ourselves when we looked in the mirror." Piper Anne's eyes fill with tears. "It makes me want to run over to Ruby and tell her that even if she was always fighting with Maple, deep down, her daughter knew her, heard her."

"Ruby is a good mom, isn't she?" I say thinking of my own in Arizona. But even before she moved she has always been so far away.

"Ruby is amazing. It makes me wish I had a mom I could talk to, a mom who would tell me I was more than enough. That *I* was a miracle."

I reach out and take Piper Anne's hand, not knowing how to comfort her. She wipes her tears with the back of her free hand. "It made me scared for Maple. She may have been in a bad place with her mom, but she would never have run away. She loved her mom even if she didn't always understand her. She had to have been taken."

"And she had plans too," I say.

"Yeah," Piper Anne nods. "Maple and I were going to go to the same college, and eventually we wanted to be roaming in the streets of France or London or Rome, having a whole life that was so much bigger than Eagle Crest. Our fantasy life was basically to see the world. We knew we couldn't take a gap year out of high school. Our parents were not going to be cool with that, and that was fine. We would plan accordingly. We had enough time to figure it out, and eventually, we would get there, and we would be free." Piper Anne cries harder now, looking at me. "But now, will we? Or will I be by myself, living out that fantasy?"

I wasn't going to give up hope. I reach for the old phone we've been using to try to break into Maple's Snap account. I type in her handle, @Maplesyrupsweetie and then I type in the passcode. "It worked."

The app opens and loads, and I see her chats, and there hasn't been any activity in days. But at the top, there's a name I don't recognize.

I click on it, and there's no hiding who it is. He sent her a video, a clip of himself: "Hey, it was so good to see you. I've been thinking about you ever since I got the email, and I'm glad you reached out; I really am. But I also want to be sure that this is the best thing for all of us. I'm thinking maybe we should talk to your mom. What do you think?"

The video is a man who looks about my dad's age. He's a little more scruffy. Longer hair. He has tattoos on his hand, and when he was talking, I couldn't help but notice the letters on his fingers: Cory. C-O-R-Y. I don't know who that is.

The message underneath it is a Snapback, and I wonder why her settings are to save all of these Snaps, but right now, I'm glad it's that, because her response is telling.

"Who is that?" Piper Anne asks, looking at the screen.

Maple replied to him. "*I loved seeing you, and I want to tell my brother and my mom, but I'm not ready yet. Can it be our secret?*"

He typed a message back: "*I don't really want to do secrets any more, Maple. I've had a lifetime of them.*"

"*What do you want to do, then?*"

"*I don't want to mess up.*"

"*Well, I want to know you.*"

My heart pounds as I read the texts. Piper Anne is shocked too, she grips my hand even tighter.

"*Well, I want to know you, too, but . . .*"

"*What?*" she replied. "*Then let's meet up again. You can teach me all the things that dads teach their kids.*"

I look at Piper Anne. "You think Cory is really her dad?"

Piper Anne nods. "It seems like it. She is wanting him to teach her dad things."

We turn our eyes back to the phone screen.

"*Like what?*" Cory asked. "*I'm guessing you already know how to ride a bike.*"

"*Well, what do you like to do?*"

"*Throw a football, play catch?*"

"*Those are things my brother would like.*"

"*All right, we could go to the movies. I could take you to ice cream.*"

She sent a laughing emoji. "*Okay, let's do ice cream.*"

"*All right. Next Saturday?*"

I kept scrolling through the messages. It seemed like they were seeing one another for over a month, every week.

"How had she never told me this?" Piper Anne asks. "She really kept all of this a secret? She found out who her father was, and all this time, she didn't want me to know? Why?"

"I don't know, but we need to go to the cops with this. Now."

CHAPTER 22

Huck

Rodgers is a solid enough detective. We've always gotten along, and there haven't been any warning signs in the relationship. But as I'm standing in his office now, I feel like I want to punch the guy.

"What are you talking about, no leads? Our entire job is to investigate this case until we bring Maple home."

"Maybe you're too close to it," he says. "The thing is, the other two girls, there's no sign of them. We've covered every possible interaction that they've had or encountered. We even have Lochlan's phone, there's nothing on it."

"I feel like words like those are a death sentence," I say to him, trying to understand this man whose job it is to find justice, to bring the girls home. It's like he's quit. "What's the deal?"

"Look, everything on Maple's computer is a dead end except that one email. There's nothing on there but some emails about college fairs. Nothing that brings us any closer to a potential kidnapper."

"What about the email?" I ask. "You've got to be able to get it traced to something. Has security gone through it?"

153

"Yes. They've gone through everything," Rodgers says. "Look, I'm not saying it's a cold case, but a week out, with three girls missing, and we've got nothing?"

"Try harder," I say. "That's your goddamn job."

I look at him with disgust, not willing to quit, and it's not because I care about Maple. It's because I care about keeping my word as an officer of the law. I will do anything to protect the citizens of this county. It's my life's work.

I leave the office, my phone buzzing as I walk to my car. I don't want to talk to Rodgers. He's a goddamn quitter, and that's the last thing I am.

"Hey," I say, seeing that it's Ruby. "Is everything all right?"

"No," she says. Her voice is frazzled. I can hear the tears in it. "Can you come over? It's really important, and . . ."

"Of course," I say. "Of course, I'll be there right away. I'm on my way." I end the phone call and drive straight to Ruby's place.

Before I get out of the car, I send Piper a quick text, *Hey, I'll be a little bit later for dinner. I can pick something up on the way home for us to eat.*

I shove my phone in my pocket as I get out of the car and walk up to Ruby's door. I knock on it and am startled by what I see when I walk into the living room.

"Okay. Huck, can you come upstairs?"

"Uh, sure," I say. I glance over my shoulder back at Dodge.

I walk up the stairs. I've never been up these stairs. I've never been in this part of Ruby's house. The walls are covered with paint-by-numbers, and they feel like a throwback, like a grandma would have done them. They don't seem like Ruby at all, which makes it all that more charming.

And even though this is the last thing that should be on my mind, when she walks up the stairs, it's impossible to not look at the way the jeans hug her ass. If it was a different time altogether, once we got to the landing, I would pull her to me. I would wrap my arms around her and ask if she's okay, because I sure as hell know she's not.

154

Instead, when we reach the top of the stairs, she tells me to come into her bedroom. I swallow. This does not feel like a police call. This feels like something more personal. She closes the door, and she tells me to sit.

"Where?" I ask.

"Here," she says, pointing to the bed. We sit on the edge of it, her and I, side by side.

The room is wallpapered. It looks like it was done fifty years ago. It matches the paintings, and I wonder if that's why she wanted this house. She could have bought anything, with all the money I know she has. Instead she chose a house that is filled with imperfections, everything half broken. But she's been slowly hiring contractors to fix it up, changing out the windows and the baseboards. The bedroom doesn't look like it's been touched, though. It looks like it has been taken out of another time altogether.

"Do you like this house?" I ask her.

She sighs. "I love it."

"How come?"

"It reminds me of my grandpa's house."

"Oh," I say. "Where'd your grandpa live?"

"Pennsylvania," she tells me.

"That's where you're from?"

"Yeah, actually I am."

"You're always so closed up about things like that. It's funny you're telling me now."

She shakes her head. "I have no more space for secrets." Her eyes are filled with tears, and they're green, and they're bright, and they're beautiful, and they're so damn broken.

"What happened?"

"You mean since you saw me last night sobbing?"

"Yeah. Since then."

"A lot. Too much. Everything?"

"You're sounding a little cryptic, Ruby."

She lies back on the bed, her knees dangling over it, and I follow her lead, lying like that next to her. We turn over on

155

our sides, and I don't know what's happening, but something is. Something different. Something unexpected.

"Rodgers is really bad at his job," I tell her.

"I know. You know who could do it better?"

"Who?" I ask.

"Nora."

"Really? She wanna be a detective?"

Ruby gently shakes her head. She closes her eyes and reaches for my hand, and I let her take it, and I don't know why, because we've never been like this before. This is a woman I hardly know, who's always been on the periphery because she's someone who doesn't let anyone in. But right now, she's letting me in, and so I am not going to waste this moment that's here.

"Did Nora find something? Something about Maple?" I ask, wondering if this is why this woman is so sad right now, if she found out something devastating.

She nods. The tears fall down her cheeks, and I've never seen a woman look so damn sad. Not like this. When I lost my wife, it was different. It was a car crash, and it was fast, and it was over, and I never held her hand as she said goodbye. I never looked in her eyes as her heart broke with the fact that she would never watch Piper grow up.

This is different. This is something I don't know. This is a woman falling apart before me.

"Why are you crying?" I ask her.

"Nora found out the truth."

"The truth of what?"

"The truth of me." And so then Ruby explains it from beginning to end.

Her words stun me, but I do my best to keep my emotions in check. That book she wrote, it wasn't fiction. It was an autobiographical account of her life, with names and places changed. But the horror of it was her story.

I take in her account. "I heard they're making a movie of it."

156

"Yeah," she said. "I got so much money for that. And you know what? The idea of that movie being in theaters on the big screen, played out. Oh, my God." She swallows. "It makes me want to . . ."

"What? Makes you want to what?"

"It makes me want to scream. Cry? But then it's like at least I'm making money off my past. That's better than most people who've gone through trauma. They just have to live with it. This way I can take my favorite people to the Amalfi Coast, or to Turkey, or anywhere. I can pay for my kids' college, and I can buy this house in cash, and I can do all those things because of what I've been through."

"I can't believe that's what really happened to you. And that's what Nora found out?"

"No. Well, yes, but that's not the worst of it."

"How in the hell is that not the worst of it?"

"Because, Huck," Ruby says, her voice catching, breathless, "it turns out my ex was released from prison. It turns out Dodge's dad, he's free."

I look into Ruby's eyes. Filled with fear, laced with panic, but also laced with hope, and all I want to do in the whole world is set her hope free. Let it live in the wild.

"Will you help me?" she asks. "Will you help me find my girl?"

"Yes," I promise. Because unlike Rodgers, I don't give up. I didn't when my wife died, and I'm not giving up now. No. This is when you fight.

157

CHAPTER 23

Ruby

I sit up in bed. Huck follows suit. "I have to go find him."

Huck's brow furrows. "Ruby, I don't think you should be looking for that man. Not after what he's done to you."

I swallow. I know what Huck is thinking, that my ex is going to hurt me, but if he has Maple, I'm not going to sit around and wait. "What would you do?" I ask him.

"I'm going to go to the station. I'm going to tell Rodgers everything. I'm going to take that folder of Nora's with the information she's discovered. I'm going to find this man and we're going to bust his ass. If he has Maple, then he'll pay. You don't have to worry about that."

I swallow, considering his words, knowing that his course of action is the sensible and swift one, but I also know that I'm a fighter and I haven't come this far to stop now.

What if their procedure takes too long? If going through the bureaucracy, through steps to get to my ex will be one minute too late? What then?

"All right," I tell him. Knowing it is not all right. Not even a little. Not at all. "So you'll just get in touch with me when you know something?"

He nods. "Yeah. Obviously I'll be contacting you soon. I'm going to head to the station right now."

"Thank you for coming, for being here."

"You don't have to thank me. I want to be here for you," he says. He squeezes my hand and there's an intimacy in this moment I want to lean into. And even though deep in my heart I know I'm not going to follow his plan, I appreciate how willing he is to look out for me.

We walk down the stairs and he gets the folder that Nora had left on the kitchen counter. "I'll see you soon," he tells me and he leans in, his lips brush my cheek. It's a tender gesture, one of care and I close my eyes, savoring it. He pulls away and looks in my eyes. "We're going to get her."

I nod because he's right. We are. Or I am.

I walk into the living room knowing that Dodge has lots of big feelings about everything that's come out this afternoon. "Look," I tell him, "I know you're upset with me, I know you feel like I betrayed you."

He scoffs. "I don't feel like anything." His phone rings. "It's Piper Anne," he tells me. He answers. "Yeah, sure. Okay. Yeah. All right, see you soon."

He ends the call looking at me. "She's on her way with Jude."

"Why?" I ask.

He shrugs. "I don't know. She wanted to talk."

"Don't be upset with me," I say. And even as I say it, I know the words are foolish, fraught with fear. He can be upset with me all he wants. That's his prerogative and I don't blame him. I've kept so many things from him, yet told the whole world about it. He has a right to be angry. "Just please know I did everything with good intentions."

He looks away, unable to meet my eyes and it kills me, feeling him withdraw. But before I can push him, there's a knock at the door.

I open it and see Piper Anne and Jude. "Hey, that was fast," I say. "I was just talking to your dad."

"My dad?"

"Yeah," I say. "We have a lead."

Piper and Jude follow me down the hallway to the living room where Dodge is. Jude sits down on the couch, looking at me with serious intent. "Look," he says. "We got into Maple's Snapchat." Jude hands his phone over to Dodge and I step closer wanting to read whatever it says.

"Is that him, Mom?" Dodge asks, flipping the phone toward me, showing me a photograph of Maple and a man.

Gasping at the image, I nod. He looks older, but no wiser, as if life has not been kind to him and I guess seventeen years in prison might do that to a man. "That's him," I say. I shake my head. "I haven't seen him in so long . . . The thing is," I say to Piper Anne, "That's not her dad."

"What do you mean?" she asks. "It sounds like it is."

"And maybe that's how he presented himself to her. But that's Dodge's father, not Maple's. They have different dads."

"Oh," Piper Anne says, frowning. "So maybe he's lying to her?"

"Well, maybe he's doing a lot more than that," I say. "She's been missing for two days. When was the last time they spoke in this chat?"

"Three days ago," Piper admits. "They never talk in it about themselves. It's always about where they're meeting."

"And where did they meet a few days ago?"

"Eagle Crest Park," she tells us.

I keel over, scared I might get sick. "Damn it. That was the last place on her phone location."

"I know," Piper Anne whispers. "That's why we came here. We were scared, too. Do we know any more about him?"

"Nora has found his social media," I say.

Piper Anne's phone is in her hand and she's already typing something in, looking him up. "Oh, that was easy," she says. "We just have to find where he lives."

"I have an idea." Dodge takes the phone and begins to type. He reads aloud what he sent, "This is Dodge, your son. I logged into Maple's account. I want to see you."

He presses send before I can stop him.

"Why would you do that?"

"If he has her, maybe it'll catch him off guard."

A moment later, there's typing, three dots on the screen. I press my hand in my chest, desperate to know what's going on, what he's going to say.

Oh, wow. Do you want to meet?

Very much, Dodge says. *Does now work?* He sends the message and another one comes back a few seconds later.

Hot Java Coffee in 30 minutes?

I frown. This seems too easy. "Dodge, we have to think this through."

"I'm not going alone," he says. "We're going together."

"We are?"

My boy reaches out and takes my hand. "We are family. No matter what."

Quickly, the four of us get in my car. "Maybe I should call Huck," I say.

Dodge shakes his head. "No Mom, we're doing this on our terms. Now." His determination pushes me forward and I drive my SUV the twenty minutes toward Hot Java Coffee. When we get there, I park a block away.

"Here's the plan," Dodge says. "I'm going to go in there and introduce myself and then right away, I'll say, 'This was a bad idea.' Then I'm going to come back here and we're going to follow him. Watch where he goes. Okay? That's how we're going to get to Maple."

I look at my son. "How did you make such a convincing plan so quickly?"

"Guess I'm good under pressure."

"I'm grateful for that, but Dodge, be safe."

He nods. "It's a public place, Mom. I will be okay." Dodge jumps out and tells me to just hang tight. Ten excruciating minutes later, Dodge emerges from the shop, jogging over to me. Another man exits the coffee shop and walks to a car parked across the street. I watch as he enters his vehicle, feeling sick.

I know that man.

I know him all too well. Scruffy hair and scruffy face. Familiar everything.

My hands grip my steering wheel. Dodge gets in the car. I turn on the gas and I follow.

BLAMELESS BUT BROKEN
by Ruby Clarke

CHAPTER 34

Lucy knew it was time. Beyond time. She had been in this room for over a year. She had a baby that was five months old, her belly that was getting swollen. She was definitely pregnant again and she was definitely escaping.

She couldn't bear to go through another day, another night, another moment where the door creaked open, another time where she would set Lucas in his portable crib — he had been upgraded from the basket now that he could crawl — knowing what was coming for her. Who was coming for her.

No, this needed to end. She'd been allowed showers since the baby was born, and when she would go and bathe every few days, washing her body and savoring the warm water, Lucas was now able to sit on the floor of the tub right by her. This couldn't be the place where he grew up. This was no life.

She looked at him, at his innocence and knew she needed to make a plan, an escape, because if she didn't, what would become of his life? What would become the life of the baby within her womb? She needed to get out.

It was hard to forge a way forward. How do you escape a place with only one door, with men keeping you inside? No windows to break through?

The only thing she was given was food, and even that had become less routine. The last few months, they would just drop off a bag of groceries in her room. She'd plead with them at first, "Please just let me out. Please just let us go. Think of the baby."

They couldn't, of course. They had cornered themselves too. Their options were kill her and take the kid somewhere, or kill both of them, or let her go and know that they would face trouble.

Her body was covered in bruises. She'd been beaten. Her hair was ragged. Her eyes were bloodshot. Her skin was pale. She was pregnant and malnourished.

When they would come to her, they would leave plastic grocery bags with loaves of bread and peanut butter and jelly. Sometimes she'd get lucky and there would be a plastic jar of applesauce, a half-gallon jug of juice. None of it is very substantial, but all of it she ate. She was eating for three. Lucas, the baby within her, and herself. They couldn't bring enough food in. She was constantly in a calorie deficit, and she knew it. She'd look in the mirror after her shower, her face so gaunt it was unrecognizable. The lightbulbs had burned out in the bathroom months earlier and they never replaced them, just adding to the eerie effect, the ghost-like way she felt. It was time for that to change. She needed to be fully alive.

And while someone was always in the hallway when she bathed, she did have that time alone in the bathroom, and that's where she came up with her plan.

She didn't know what the outside of the building she lived in was like. So she couldn't go all Shawshank on the situation and begin peeling back tiles in the shower and digging out dirt to make a hole, making an opening big enough to crawl though, because she didn't know where that wall led, what the bathroom was up against.

Was she in an apartment, in a house, in a basement, in a barn? Was she on a second story, a tenth story? She couldn't know. She just knew she was trapped and she needed to get out.

And one day when she was in the bathroom showering, she found her weapon, in plain sight all along.

She took two of the curtain rings holding up the shower curtain. When she dressed herself in the T-shirt they gave her, she lifted Lucas, pressed him against her body and put the two shower curtain rings between them both, pressing into her. She had no pockets, nowhere to put anything. She prayed that Lucas would stay put. "You done in there?" Romeo asked. He shoved open the door and she walked out of the bathroom. She knew these men by name now, the three of them that usually came, Romeo, Justice and Frank. She knew because they would speak to one another when they came for her, when they entered her room with that greedy look in their eyes, usually coked out or drunk, never to the point though where she could escape, but sometimes she knew that they were high and she thought if she had a weapon, she could do something while they didn't have all their wits about them.

Otherwise, they were smart. Coming in a pair or a three-some meant she never had a hope of getting the upper hand, but that was before she had the curtain rings in her room. She bent them into two long lines, on the concrete floor, she began to sharpen them, shoving the mattress aside, always on edge because what if they came while she was in the middle of sharpening her tools?

She made sure to do it right after they had their way with her, when Lucas was still asleep.

After the men would come for what they wanted, she would push the mattress aside and she would reach for the tools, sharpening them until she knew they would draw blood. She knew because she practiced on the base of her foot, and it worked. Next time they came in the room, she'd be ready.

Outside of her bedroom there was a bathroom directly to the left and beyond that there were no doors, but a short

165

hallway. She didn't think the men who came for her spent much time here.

Whatever this building was for, she didn't think someone lived here. She never smelled food being cooked or people talking or laughing in another part of the house. Still, she had no guarantees about any of this. But she wasn't looking for a guarantee. After being locked up here for over a year, it was time for these men to pay.

And while she had never fought back in the past because she was so concerned about them hurting her and in return, hurting the baby, she had been the perfect prisoner, but that was before she had two sharp objects, and she knew exactly where they were going to go.

She never knew when they would come to see her, and if it would be one, two, or all three.

When they came that night, it was two of them.

They grunted, telling her to take off her shirt. She did as they asked. She always did as they asked, she had Lucas to think about, the baby within her to consider. She was not going to cause a scene if it might mean these men, who were so much bigger than her, might do something irreparable.

They told her where to lay, to open her mouth, to part her knees, and she obliged. But while they were forcing her into acts without her consent, she reached for the sharpened points nestled against the side of her mattress. The men were so lost in the moment and getting what they wanted, that they didn't realize what she was doing.

She went after Romeo, the man on top of her, first, with all of her might. She took one of the rods and jabbed it in his neck against the jugular.

Frank, who was preparing himself to fill her next, began screaming, "What the hell? What's going on?"

Because at that point, blood was spurting everywhere.

Romeo was falling back, his hand against his neck, blood gushing. She knew she only had one moment and she wouldn't hesitate.

As Frank looked at Romeo in horror, and then down at her, she leapt for him.

Two points in her hand, one wrapped in each fist, and she jabbed him in the neck as well. She knew she needed the weapons in case she came across anyone else while she was running out of this room. She gripped them tight in her hands.

Frank fell back, yelling at her, but blood spurting, his eyes spinning back, and she scrambled out of the bed, ran for Lucas, picked him up. He was scared and began screaming, but Romeo and Frank's voices drowned out the child's cries.

She yanked open the door and she ran down the hall.

She passed the bathroom, and got to an open room, in the corner there was a large safe. There were tables there filled with bags of cocaine, and pills. This was where they moved product.

That made sense. Someone might be here sleeping on the couch, keeping watch on her and the goods, but no one lived here, not like she had.

The men were calling for her. She looked behind her and saw Frank crawling, but he was going to pass out. She knew it. There was so much blood coating her body, her skin and now Lucas too. She was naked, raw, bloody and bare.

But she pulled open the door and she was free.

It was a warehouse, she realized as she walked outside, turning in a circle to find her bearings. The sun was high in the sky. It was daytime. She was so glad that it wasn't night.

Her feet were bare, but she knew how to run even though it had been so long since she stretched her legs. "Lucas," she whispered, "We're going to be okay. We're going to be okay."

She knew they would be, because there was no other choice. She was going to be free, and so were her babies.

They ran until she saw a woman walking to her car, parked on the side of the street. The woman was older, black hair with silver streaks.

"Help," Lucy screamed, "Help!"

"Oh my God," the woman said, looking at her. "Are you okay?"

"No," Lucy sobbed. "The men in there, they held me hostage. I need the police. I need 9-1-1. Help, help!"

The woman didn't panic. She reached for her cell phone in her pocket, pressed 9-1-1, and whatever she said into that phone, Lucy didn't know, but the woman ended the call a moment later and reached in her trunk for a blanket and wrapped it around Lucy's shoulders. Lucy's body shook. The woman opened her passenger side door and she eased Lucy into it. It could have been thirty seconds or thirty minutes, she didn't know. But soon sirens were blaring, barreling toward them. Police cars arrived, a fire truck, an ambulance.

The rest of that day was a blur. She was in a hospital room when she woke up.

A nurse came in, Lucas was in her arms against her chest, she clung to him.

"You're awake miss?" Lucy nodded. "What's your name? Everybody's been wanting to know."

"I'm Lucy Callahan," she whispered, "and I need the police."

"They're here," the nurse said. "Do you need anything, water?"

"No, I just need a police officer right now." Lucy was shaking, but she knew what she needed to say.

Two officers came in, a man and a woman. They looked at her with wide-eyed expressions. "You're awake," the woman officer said.

Lucy nodded. She may have gone into a stress state when she ran out of that building, but she was alert right now, she was present.

"Did they survive?" she asked. "Romeo and Frank?"

"No, both the men were dead on arrival."

Lucy nodded. "There's two other men," she said. "One is Justice, I don't know his last name, but he would come for me too."

168

"Come for you?" they asked.

She nodded, "Yes, I've been in that room for over a year. I gave birth to Lucas there. I know I'm pregnant again. They tortured me." She could feel the tension in the room as the officers absorbed her story, and even though they must have surmised something from the scene at that warehouse, the details were horrific. "But there's one other person besides Justice who needs to pay. He's the reason I'm there."

"Who," the officer asked.

"His name is Knox Favor, and he owed them money. He didn't have the cash," Lucy said her voice soft. The realization just beginning to dawn on her, she was free. "Knox Favor is the reason this has happened, he's the reason for all of this."

169

CHAPTER 24

Jude

"You should call your father," Ruby says to Piper Anne as she starts the car to follow Cory to the next location. "Or I will."

Piper Anne and I keep looking at each other. Piper Anne shakes her head. "Not yet."

I see Ruby bite her lip. I understand. None of this feels right. Through the rear-view mirror I see worry in her eyes.

"Do you want me to drop you off at the police station?"

"No," Piper Anne says quickly. "Don't drop us off. I want to find Maple."

"Your dad's going to kill me if I take you there," she says.

"Just leave them in the car, Mom. Me and you, we'll go to his place," Dodge says. "Besides, if we go to the station, we will lose him. Look, he's turning left. Go!" Dodge shouts, cutting his mom off.

She makes a quick turn and continues to follow the car that Cory is driving to a small house in a part of town I never go to.

Cory gets out of the car and walks to the front door of an old home on a corner lot.

"What did you say to him?" she asks Dodge.

Dodge shrugs. "I said, this was a bad idea, I don't think I can do this."

"What did you think when you saw him face to face?"

"I thought it was weird. Like how is that my dad? And then I was thinking about the book you wrote and then I kind of got overwhelmed and I just wanted to get back to the car. I didn't want to do it. How did Maple do it?"

"Maybe Maple didn't know the whole story. Otherwise, why would she have contacted him?"

"Maybe Maple figured it out," Piper Anne says softly. "Maybe she picked up the clues that you dropped in the book, realizing it was your own life before anybody else did."

Tears fill Ruby's eyes.

"What, Mom?" Dodge asks. "What are you thinking?"

"If that's the case," she says, "then maybe my daughter knew me better than I thought. Maybe she does know me best of all." She parks opposite Cory's house, unbuckles her seatbelt and gets out of the car. Dodge follows her, and then Piper Anne and I are alone. Whatever Ruby and Dodge are about to find, we are only going to hear second hand.

Fear courses through me. "You think she's in there?"

"I don't know. But if she is, I'm scared." She pauses. "You know, I might not have a mom who knows me better than anybody else, but I do have a dad."

I watch as Piper Anne calls his number. He picks up right away. Of course, he does.

"Piper, you okay?"

"No, Daddy," she tells him. "No, Daddy, I'm not. I need you to come here. I need you to come here now."

CHAPTER 25

Ruby

He's not expecting me, that much is clear. But when he pulls open the door and sees my face, it's like we've both gone back in time.

"Holy shit. Tilly," he says, looking at me. "Well, it's Ruby now, huh? Ruby Clarke?"

"Is she in here?" I plead. "Is Maple in here?"

"What? What are you talking about?"

"I know you've been talking to her. I've seen the texts. On Snapchat, I saw your conversation. I know you have her."

"She's not in here, Tilly, I swear. I swear to you I'm not lying."

"Where is she? She's been gone for two days."

"What? What are you talking about? Gone where?"

"I don't know," I say. "But if she's in here and you have hurt her, I swear to God . . . Do you have the other girls too? Lochlan? And Brittany? Are they here?" I push past him. Cory lifts his hands up as if in defense.

Dodge is behind me walking into the house. "Mom," he says, "calm down."

"Calm down?" I push past both of them and I walk into the home. Pulling open the bathroom door, pushing back the shower curtain, it's empty. There's two bedrooms, one on opposite sides of each other. Both of the doors are open. One has a queen-size mattress on the floor, nobody is in the room. The other room has a weight bench and some dumbbells.

There's a kitchen. I storm through the house, circle it. "Is there a basement," I ask. "Are the girls in the basement? Is that where you have the girls?"

"I don't have the girls," Cory says. "I don't. I don't know where Maple is. I don't know what you're talking about. I haven't heard from her in days and then Dodge texts me on her phone and I'm confused and then he doesn't want to talk and I don't know what's happening." Cory is shouting now, but I'm shouting too.

"I don't give a damn about you knowing what's happening. All I care about is knowing where my baby is. Where is she? Where is she?" I want to wrap my fingers around his neck. I want that bent shower curtain ring to jab in his neck and make him bleed out.

Just the same as Romeo and Frank all those years ago. And maybe I'm a monster and maybe it's always been there under the surface. And maybe writing out my story didn't get all the anger I had for that year out on paper. But I don't have a weapon in my hand and I'm not going to reach for a knife in the kitchen. Instead, I run out of the house and around to the back. There's steps and a door leading to an exterior basement. I kick it open but it's cold and it's empty, and there's a washing machine and a dryer that look about thirty years old. There are cobwebs and a basket of dirty laundry and nothing else. It's small and it's empty and there are no missing girls. No one is here. No one, no one.

"Where is Maple?" I run out of the laundry room back around the house and by now Piper and Jude and Huck are in the front yard. When did the cops arrive?

"Ruby," Huck says "Ruby."

"Don't Ruby me," I say, "This man is a monster and he has my daughter."

"Maybe he doesn't," Huck says.

"I swear to you," Cory says hands in the air. "I haven't done a thing."

Detective Rodgers is here too, I see, getting out of his car. There're two other cop cars as well. Four cars in all.

"Who called the cops? I thought we were doing this on our own?"

"Sorry," Piper Anne says. "I had to. Ruby, I had to."

I'm shaking and crying and scared, but I haven't come this far to stop now.

"Why are you here?" I ask Cory, "Why did you come back and start talking to my daughter?"

"I came into town because I was going to talk to you. I thought, eventually, I would get the courage to talk to you. After everything," he says. "After everything we've been through."

"*We've* been through nothing," I seethe, refusing to give him an inch of me.

"That's not true. This boy right here is my son and I deserve to know him."

"You deserve nothing," I say. "You shouldn't even be out of prison. You should be in there for life."

"No," he says. "I shouldn't because I didn't hurt you. Not like they did and you know I didn't think that they were going to kidnap you. I never knew."

"What did you think was going to happen?"

"It wasn't like that." Cory says, "I tried to find you. I thought you ran off. I thought you left out of fear."

"You thought I'd just disappear in the middle of the night?"

"Yes," he says, "And why wouldn't you? You find out your boyfriend is a drug dealer and mixed up with all that shady shit. You're pregnant. You're smart. You knew to get away. That's what I thought. At least."

"I wasn't going to leave you. I loved you."

174

"Why? I was always a dirt bag. I was never good enough for you."

I look at him, wanting to be furious, not knowing what to believe, but none of it matters because right now Maple is still gone.

Maple, my Maple. I have to find her. "Why did you want to see Maple? She isn't your daughter."

"What did you want me to say to her?" he asks. "She knows I'm not her dad. She realizes the book was true. She wanted a connection. I gave her one. Everybody's looking for some hope, Ruby."

"No," I say, "I don't want to hope. All I'm looking for is a miracle."

"Hey," Piper Anne says, "maybe I found your miracle."

I look over at her and she hands me the phone. "I've been looking through her Snaps and there's one other person I don't know. Do you know who this is, Jude? @DocNeedsNurse."

I take the phone from her, reading.

"You were a good patient today." My stomach rolls over.

"I'm surprised to see you on Snapchat," Maple wrote back.

"I wanted to check in on my favorite patient. I've always been looking out for you."

"I know," she says. "In Italy, you weren't just looking out for me. You were looking *at* me."

I want to vomit, but I keep reading.

"I can't help it. You're so beautiful."

"Is that what you thought when I came in today to get my vaccine?"

"It's what I've always thought."

"This seems wrong." Maple says.

"Does it feel wrong? Because how we feel is what matters."

Oh my God, I want to kill him. This cannot be happening. Just like the shower curtain rings were a weapon in plain sight, so is my daughter's kidnapper.

"I know who this is."

175

"Me, too," Piper Anne says, her eyes welling with tears.

"It's Tom. Nora's husband. He was in Italy. He is a doctor." I look at Huck. "I don't know where he might be. The girls couldn't be at Nora's, there's no way. There's no way." I look at Huck. He's already talking to Detective Rodgers.

"We need someone at Dr. Campbell's residence." He's speaking into a walkie-talkie. "They're moving now," he says as he looks at me. "Don't call Nora. We can't rule anything out. She may have had something to do with this."

"No, no." I say, "It's not possible."

I look back at the messages. They've been talking for about a week and then they said, "Let's meet up on the last day of school."

I look over at Cory. "Did you go with Maple to Eagle Crest Park?"

He nods. "Yeah. I was with her there on the last day of school. I picked her up. She said she wanted to talk about something. And I know it's wrong of me to have picked her up from school but she seemed upset. We went to the park, but then she clammed up. She wouldn't tell me what she was thinking about. When I said that it felt like we were crossing lines, that I should talk to you if we were going to hang out anymore, she got mad."

Cory ran a hand on the back of his neck. "I know I'm a piece of shit." He looks at Huck, "And I get it. I'm probably going back to jail. For something, I don't know, for being sketchy? Regardless, I left the park and she stayed."

I look at Huck, "And then Tom came."

"Don't call Nora," he repeats. "In case she's involved. We can't tip her off."

But I know he's wrong. "Nora's not involved."

"You can't be sure of anything," he says. "Not in a time like this. Your judgment might be . . ."

"No." I say, "Nora was helping me find whoever did this to Maple. She was sure it was Cory."

"Well, that would've been a good cover."

"No, I can trust her." My mind goes back to the day Maple went missing. Nora and Tom came straight to the house. I tell this to Huck.

"What did Tom say that day?"

I press a finger to the bridge of my nose, trying to think. "He said that he'd just come from Juniper Lane."

"But what's over there?" Huck asks.

"The duplex he owns. He said he had been there to fix a plumbing issue . . . but what if . . . What if he was keeping one of the apartments? What if . . . ?" I cover my mouth. "I'm getting in my car," I say dashing to my Subaru.

Dodge gets in the car with me, and even though Huck and Officer Rodgers are telling me to stop, I press the gas. We leave Piper Anne with her dad. Jude too. I drive. Maybe it's wrong. Maybe I should have the police with me, but I don't care. Right now. All I care about is getting my daughter.

I drive to the duplex. Dodge telling me to drive faster, all the while asking, "Are you okay?"

"I'm not okay." I say, "But I am getting my daughter."

"Mom," he says, "You know how you're always looking for miracles? Maybe you are her miracle."

I exhale, knowing that all of us are miracles.

We're still standing despite all of the shit we've been through. Dads who left us, parents who died, grandpa's having a heart attack in the front seat of the Dodge pickup truck.

All of it heartbreaking. All of it life.

But the ones who are here, who are still standing, we are the miracle. We are love, and we can't let the darkness of the world take away any of our light.

Not now, not ever.

CHAPTER 26

Ruby

Pulling up to the duplex, my chest is tight, my heart pounds, everything is constricted, and I find that I'm gripping the steering wheel.

Dodge rests a hand on my arm. "It's gonna be okay. Whatever we find inside there."

"All that matters is Maple." I practically leap out of the car, keeping the keys in the ignition. I don't even know if I turned it off. All I know is that my feet are moving me forward, faster.

I hear police cars in the distance, parking, officers behind me, but in that moment, I am already at the front door kicking at it.

"Open, open," I scream, my fists tight as my fury.

There's no answer. I suppose there wouldn't be. If Tom truly has Maple inside this house, he wouldn't willingly open the door.

I can't wait. There's a window next to the door and I kick it in with my foot, glass flying, Dodge behind me. "Mom, are you okay?"

"No," I say, shrieking, reaching my hand through the broken glass to unlock the door. I yank it open. I'm inside. I start to shout. "Maple? Maple?"

I don't see Tom anywhere, but I see a sickening scene. Metal chairs in the living room. It's not furnished like an apartment.

There's a tripod and cameras. I feel sick. It's a film set. There are sets of handcuffs on the floor. I see items used for sex acts. I clench my jaw. Even if Maple isn't here, whatever is happening here does not feel okay.

"Maple?" I scream. "Maple? Lochlan? Brittany?"

And then I hear a voice.

"Mom? Mom? Mom?"

I run down the hall. It's a small duplex, but in that instant I have a memory of myself running down a hall as I left that warehouse all those years ago, pressing Dodge against my chest, my womb swollen with Maple.

I was naked and bare, but not broken.

I got out alive with my children. And I found freedom. And I made the men who hurt me pay. And now I will set my daughter free.

I see heavy locks on the door, keeping the girls inside.

"Mom, help."

I kick on the door. I slam on it with my body, full force. Dodge is here at my side, just like he was when he was a newborn and we were alone in a room on a mattress together. He saved me, literally. I don't think I could have got through that horror if I hadn't had my baby boy to hold tight.

And he's with me now, and he kicks at the door, his weight and strength cracking it open and there she is.

As the door breaks free, Maple is sitting on the floor, her hands and feet bound, propped against the wall.

Brittany and Lochlan lie in the fetal position. They're in nothing but T-shirts. They look exhausted, their eyes filled with tears.

But also filled with hope.

They know they're getting out alive.

Behind me is Huck, Detective Rodgers, a whole squad, but I don't pay attention to what they're doing and how they're moving throughout the building.

This is Tom's house. He's a respected pediatrician in this town and it's probably how he was able to get to Lochlan and Brittany.

The thought makes me sick. What a twisted world we live in.

I've known it for so long, but I think since I moved here and started my new life I pushed the horror of how sick people can be out of my mind. Now, I can't run from it.

I fall down at Maple's feet. "Oh, baby," I say. "Oh, baby, you're here. I thought I lost you." My fingers unfurl the knots and Detective Rodgers pulls out a small knife, helping release the girls one at a time.

The whole complex swarms with people, sirens in the distance, a fire truck blaring down the street. I hope Lochlan and Brittany's parents are already on their way. They knew to hold on to hope. Now, I will never let the flame of hope die. All we need to survive is a flicker.

All of that noise, everything around me disappears as I simply wrap my arms around my baby girl and I pull her to me and she cries against my chest, sobbing. I can imagine better than most what she has been through. The clues in the living room tell me that whatever's been done to her and Brittany and Lochlan for the last few days will be etched in their memories for the rest of their lives.

"Tom did this," she whispers. "Tom did this to all of us. I thought, I thought he was, I thought he wanted me. It felt good. I thought he loved me. And I was confused . . . I met Dodge's dad and got angry and Tom said I was special and . . . I'm so stupid . . . I'm so sorry."

"Don't apologize, love, you are safe, that is all that matters," I say, and it is because she's a child, and Tom is a grown man who is twisted and perverted and taking advantage of impressionable children. He is a monster.

Lochlan and Brittany stand and I feel like I want to wrap them up in a blanket and hold them tight. An EMT seems to read my mind because the girls are given blankets, draping them around their bodies so their bare legs are no longer exposed. And I wrap Maple's blanket around her shoulders, pulling her tight against me again.

"Oh, sweetie," I say, "I'm so glad you are in my arms."

She sobs against me. Her head buried in my shoulder. "I wanted to know who my dad was, and I put pieces together, once I figured out the truth, I didn't know how to say it. You had been through so much, and I'm sorry for that, Mom. You are so brave. And so strong, but talking about it all felt like too much."

And that is the truth. It is too much. All of this, each one of us just trying to grow up and survive.

The fact any of us do it at all is a miracle.

CHAPTER 27

Ruby

Three months later, I type the words *The End* on the final page of my new manuscript.

I press save, relief and pride washing through me as I lean back in my desk chair looking out the window, the water of the Puget Sound before me. The current is fast and flowing, the kind you could get swept away in if you weren't careful.

I think about the book I just completed. How I'm selling it as fiction once again, even though it is a true account. The truth is all about perspective anyways, we would all tell the story differently. This is just how I am telling mine. And I have made peace that that is the kind of writer I am, actually. Taking my real-life experiences and putting them on the page and hoping that they connect with someone somewhere.

I am filled with nothing but gratitude that everybody else doesn't have to live through the horrors I faced, that my children have faced.

When I told my editor that I was actually going to be writing a sequel to *Broken But Blameless*, she was surprised.

"Really?" she said. "I thought the story kind of ended. Where does it pick up?"

I told her it picks up seventeen years later. That Lucy and her two children, who were now grown, found themselves wrapped up in the story from all those years ago. Knox was released from prison. Lucas was in college, and the daughter that hadn't been born yet at the end of the first novel was just finishing her junior year of high school when she gets kidnapped.

My editor was impressed. "Okay, I love it," she said. "What happens?"

Over a video chat, I filled her in about the rest of the story. It was all lifted from my life. Only this time I had permission from my children to share what had happened to them. I wasn't sure they would want me to, but their bravery amazed me.

Maple had insisted I write this book. "Mom," she says, "use everything we've gone through for something good."

Dodge agreed. "I just hope that whatever we go through next isn't as bad because we really don't need a part three."

I couldn't agree more with that sentiment. I never want to lose my children again. If I ever write another story, maybe this time it will be a romance. A book about me finding real love for the first time in my life.

Getting permission to write the book from Nora led to a trickier conversation. She came over one morning for coffee. We sat at my kitchen table. Her eyes were heavy, circles under them. Her hair needed to be washed. She was in leggings and a sweatshirt. She looked like she'd aged five years in five weeks.

After I proposed the concept of the novel, she looked at me thoughtfully. "Why the hell not?" She finally said.

"Are you sure? Tom was your husband and—"

"You'll change his name and maybe instead of a doctor, he can be a dentist or something. I don't know. It doesn't really matter, Ruby. He's going to be in prison for the rest of his life. The divorce has been filed. It's over. I thought he was someone he maybe never was."

"You didn't ever suspect him of—"

"No," she says. "I didn't suspect anything, but now we know the truth, don't we?" And we did. After Tom was arrested, they began going through his computers and the damaging information found was more than heartbreaking. He had been photographing minors for the entirety of his career as a doctor.

Nora swore she had no clue, and I believed her. She wanted me to find Maple, she had been a faithful friend to me since the day we met. She had no idea that the duplex that they bought was being used for this.

"I never thought of going there," she told me. "He was the property manager. What was I going to do? Go fix the dishwasher? No, it wasn't even on my radar, it was never on my mind to go check out the renters. I thought it was just a long-term investment. The fact that he bought it with that intent . . ." She shook her head, tears in her eyes, disturbed by the magnitude of her husband's depravity.

With permission granted, I sat down at my computer, writer's block gone, and I spent three months writing out the story that had only spanned a few days. A heartbreaking account of Maple being kidnapped on that last day of school . . . and everything that unfolded after.

Now, I quickly type up an email. "This is the first draft. Be as harsh as possible," I tell my editor before attaching the file and hitting send.

I stand from my computer chair and I lift my hands to the ceiling, stretching. My body feels sore, but in a good way. I finished the book, the book I didn't think I could even write.

I head downstairs. Senior year would be starting in a few days for Maple, and Dodge will head back to college. And my life was evolving in even more ways.

In the kitchen, Huck is standing at the counter. "So," he says, looking at me with a big smile. "Did you finish?"

I step toward him. I don't give him a hug because he has both hands in a stainless-steel bowl of chicken thighs that he is marinating.

Instead, on my tippy toes, I lean up, and I kiss him quickly. "A man who knows how to handle meat is pretty sexy," I say with a laugh.

Then I slap his butt and open the refrigerator, reaching for a can of sparkling water.

"Nora, Piper, and Jude are going to be here in about an hour," he tells me. "I'm going to grill this chicken, and I put together a pasta salad. It's in the fridge."

"Wow," I say, cracking open the can and taking a sip. "I really love that you know how to cook."

He chuckles. "This isn't complicated. It's some meat on a grill."

"Still," I say. "I like having you around, Huck."

"You do?" He looks over at me. With the chicken done, he walks to the sink and begins to wash his hands. He dries them off on a paper towel and then steps back to me. "Piper says that we can't move in together until she graduates high school next year."

I smile. "That's fair. I feel like there's no reason to rush it."

Huck smiles at me. "I agree," he says. "Why rush things when we have the rest of our lives to spend together?"

Maple walks into the kitchen through the back door. "Hey, guys. Sorry, am I interrupting?" she asks with a laugh. She drops her tote bag on the kitchen table. She's in her uniform from the country club.

"How did work go?" I ask her.

She grins. "I made $42 in tips, which is pretty good for one shift."

"Yeah, it is," I say.

"And how did your work day go?" she asks.

"Thanks for asking," I say. "I finished the book."

Her eyes widen. "Good, because we're having a celebratory dinner. If you didn't meet your deadline, that would've been awkward."

I chuckle. "Okay. No pressure, right?"

"Well, you met the pressure, so I think you're good, Mom. Does it feel good to be finished?"

I nod, feeling emotion swell within me. "It feels incredible. Also, it feels a little bit like closure I wasn't expecting."

Huck places the chicken in the refrigerator. "Are you glad Cory moved out of state?"

I nod. "Very glad. I understand why he wanted to come and see us. See me. But that's my past and I want to keep it there."

* * *

Later when we're sitting down at the table outside for dinner with our garden lights strung up across the patio, I look at my family and friends.

Jude and Piper and Maple are laughing about something, an inside joke, and I'm glad that the three of them have one another. If a beginning of a relationship had sparked earlier this spring between Maple and Jude, it's faded now. Instead, the three of them have cemented themselves as best friends. I'm thankful that they have each other going into their last year of high school. It gives me hope that better times are ahead.

Nora looks at me from across the table. "How are you doing?" she asks.

"I've never been happier," I admit. And she smiles at me. "Me too. Who'd have thought my husband needed to go to prison in order for me to feel free."

I know what she means. We've talked about it a lot over the last few months. How, although she felt like her marriage was satisfactory, there was never deep passion, had been years of feeling alone, going through the motions, her needs not being met. Now she was free to find out who she wanted to be in this next chapter of her life.

Looking around the table, my heart is full in ways I truly never expected for myself and makes me miss my grandpa. I wish he was here, but maybe he is. I feel warmth around me and I think he would be proud of the woman I've become.

I smile, thinking that this moment, right here in my backyard, feels so safe, so tender. There's no warning signs, no red flags cropping up when I look at the people around me. It's more than miraculous. It's being fully alive.

THE END

THE JOFFE BOOKS STORY

We began in 2014 when Jasper agreed to publish his mum's much-rejected romance novel and it became a bestseller.

Since then we've grown into the largest independent publisher in the UK. We're extremely proud to publish some of the very best writers in the world, including Joy Ellis, Faith Martin, Caro Ramsay, Helen Forrester, Simon Brett and Robert Goddard. Everyone at Joffe Books loves reading and we never forget that it all begins with the magic of an author telling a story.

We are proud to publish talented first-time authors, as well as established writers whose books we love introducing to a new generation of readers.

We won Trade Publisher of the Year at the Independent Publishing Awards in 2023. We have been shortlisted for Independent Publisher of the Year at the British Book Awards for the last four years, and were shortlisted for the Diversity and Inclusivity Award at the 2022 Independent Publishing Awards. In 2023 we were shortlisted for Publisher of the Year at the RNA Industry Awards.

We built this company with your help, and we love to hear from you, so please email us about absolutely anything bookish at feedback@joffebooks.com

If you want to receive free books every Friday and hear about all our new releases, join our mailing list: www.joffebooks. com/contact

And when you tell your friends about us, just remember: it's pronounced Joffe as in coffee or toffee!

www.ingramcontent.com/pod-product-compliance
Lightning Source LLC
Chambersburg PA
CBHW011434170626
46808CB00010B/3151